THE CROWNLESS PRINCE

THE CROWNLESS PRINCE
Copyright © 2023 Selina R. Gonzalez.
ALL RIGHTS RESERVED.

This book or any portion thereof may NOT be reproduced or
redistributed electronically or manually, uploaded to any server, uploaded
to or crawled for use in any A.I. or text generation training dataset, or
used in any manner whatsoever without the express written permission of
the publisher/author except for the use of brief quotations in a book
review. Please contact author with merchandizing requests.

All characters in this book are fictional. Any resemblance to persons living
or dead, events, or locales is purely coincidental.

ISBN: 978-1-957499-10-9

Cover Design by Selina R. Gonzalez

Published by Wyvern Wing Press
htttp://www.WyvernWingPress.com
https://www.SelinaRGonzalez.com

AEDYLLAN CHRONICLES

THE CROWNLESS PRINCE

SELINA R. GONZALEZ

Also available from Selina R. Gonzalez

The Miraveld Chronicles

For more adventures in Aedyllan and other kingdoms in
the continent of Miraveld, set about 200 years after
The Crownless Prince.

A Thieving Curse (A *Beauty and the Beast* reimagining)
A Lonely Dance (A *Twelve Dancing Princesses* reimagining)
A Fated Quest (A *Golden Bird* reimagining)
A Stolen Heart (A *Goose Girl* reimagining)

*Dedicated to the C-dramas
that helped keep me sane
in 2022, and to their
stellar wigs that inspired
me to give Aedyllanian
men long hair.*

Map of

Miraveld

Nydellan
Principality
Aedyllan
Alimer
Principality
aine
incipality
nlae

The Kingdom of Aedyllan

List of principalities and their rulers:

Alimer Principality — Prince Arlius Alimer
Father of Prince Marcus Alimer

Faine Principality — Prince Mortimer Faine
Father of Princess Adriana Faine

Nydellan Principality — Prince Uldrich Nydellan

PROLOGUE

In the fading light, the looming stone tower cast a long shadow, as if trying to swallow up the small procession moving toward it. The flickering orange glow of the torches offered no comfort.

Prince Marcus eyed the few, recently barred windows in the square tower. He hadn't thought his father so serious about his threat. Realizing how easily his father, the current ruler of Alimer Principality, would imprison his youngest son, and at only seventeen, only made him respect the man less.

Their procession reached the tower, and a stone-faced guardsman opened the door.

"Marcus."

He turned to face his father, his teeth clenching. Torchlight gleamed on the thin gold crown resting on Prince Arlius's dark hair and cast the angles of his face in harsh contrast.

"This is your final chance. Repent and accept the marriage I've arranged for you."

Even if things were different, Marcus had no desire for a

loveless marriage designed to secure a military alliance. He would not aid his father in plotting against the other two sovereign Aedyllanian principalities and hastening war. The union his father wanted symbolized the opposite of the dream he shared with Adriana—of a peaceful Aedyllan without all of this vying for power.

Tipping up his chin, he looked his father in the eyes. "I love Princess Adriana Faine. I gave her my vow. I will marry her and none other."

His father's expression contorted. "Idiotic fool of a disloyal son! Let's see if a few years of seclusion will teach you respect and understanding of your allegiances! Enter the tower."

Marcus glanced at the guards surrounding them, then his gaze fell on Edwin, whose head was bowed to avoid drawing attention to himself. He turned back to his father. "I ask you again to reconsider Edwin's—"

"This ungrateful dog lied for you, covered for you, and assisted you in defying me," his father bellowed. "Would you rather I have him executed for treason?"

Marcus took a step back, toward the tower, his stomach dropping. Surely he wouldn't . . . would he? "No, Father."

"If they won't enter, force them in."

At the regnant prince's order, a couple of guards stepped toward them. Marcus grabbed Edwin's sleeve and dragged his servant-guard into the tower after him. The door slammed shut, plunging them into darkness, and a lock clicked.

His father's command came muffled through the thick wood. "Plaster over the door!"

Marcus swallowed. The craftsmen his father had brought along would close up the only door into the tower, and then his father would impress his seal into the drying plaster, so no Alimer subject would dare to break it. The other principalities would not challenge that seal within Alimer territory, either, so even Adriana's father, Prince Mortimer, couldn't help Marcus if he wanted to.

How could they escape? The door was thick, and the plaster would be, too. The stone walls were even thicker. Would the bars in the windows prove an easier obstacle? The biggest challenge would be going unnoticed, so their progress wasn't thwarted. Perhaps they could tear up the floorboards and dig their way out.

A small part of him still hoped this was a ruse. Surely when his father realized how serious Marcus was, he would relent. The door would be opened, and his father would say, "You truly are a man of your word. I cannot punish you for that."

Instead, scraping sounded on the outside of the door.

"I'll look for a light, my lord," Edwin murmured. His footsteps moved away, further into the dark tower, but Marcus stood rooted in place, listening to the sound of his freedom ending.

Was his father watching impassively? Did he care at all that he was losing his youngest son? Would he really leave Marcus there for seven years? They'd never been close, as Marcus didn't share his father's aggressive nature and would rather wait for peaceable solutions to disagreements. Still, his father's callous treatment cut him deeply.

Then there were his two elder brothers. Neither had accompanied them, and both had called him foolish in the past. Did they agree with their father that seven years of isolation was what he deserved for not supporting their father's kingship aspirations?

A curse upon the last king of Aedyllan, who had died nearly a century prior without heirs. In his *infinite* wisdom, King Vithmir had thought appointing his three most trusted friends as equal princes would prevent a power struggle. Now those princes' great-great-grandsons did little but argue and were all eyeing the title of *king*. And Marcus, for daring to believe the principalities could continue to coexist and having the audacity to fall in love with the daughter of a man his father considered a rival, was being punished for a long-dead king's lack of foresight.

The minutes dragged by. Edwin returned with candles and left one on the floor when Marcus made no move to take it. Cold seeped into his fingers and toes, the winter chill not yet fully driven away by the emergence of spring. Still he stood, unmoving.

Eventually, the scraping stopped. Voices said something he couldn't make out.

Then his father's authoritative voice. "I seal this tower with my mark and a fae curse."

Marcus jolted.

"This tower will be impervious to harm, unable to be broken into or out of, until I order it opened, or I perish."

Marcus staggered back. His father was so angry he'd risked seeking aid from the dangerous fae to keep Marcus incarcerated?

Any remaining cords of familial affection or loyalty snapped.

He'd be trapped here.

For seven years.

With no escape.

"Adriana . . ." Her name left his lips like a plea as his heart shattered. His knees gave out, and he dropped to the floor, tears blurring his vision. "I'm sorry."

He'd made her a promise.

"I'll always love you. I don't care how long we have to wait for our fathers to see past their pride; I won't give up on the dream of us and of peace. One day, Adriana, I'll marry you. I swear it, on the stars in the sky and the blood in my veins and the ancient soil beneath my feet. I'll be your husband."

"Forgive me," Marcus whispered.

And then he curled up on the floor next to the faltering candle and wept over the death of dreams.

CHAPTER 1

"Stop fretting." Marcus sat on the forest floor, intent on weaving together the wildflowers he'd picked. Spring had arrived early, and although the chilly air still necessitated thicker tunics and trousers, at least the snow was gone and the flowers blooming. "I'll be fine if you do your part."

From atop his horse, Edwin scowled. "I shouldn't leave you alone."

"You want to protect me?" Marcus picked up the last long-stemmed flower, weaving it in with the others. That looked like enough. "Go hunt something so Father doesn't question what I was doing when we return."

Truthfully, he was tired of lying and sneaking around, but the alternative was outright defying his father, and he wasn't ready for that confrontation. Not yet. Maybe never, an accusing part of him whispered, but he ignored it.

"Your Highness—"

Hoofbeats sounded nearby, approaching them in a hurry. Marcus quickly tied the woven chain of flowers into a loop and scrambled to his feet, hiding the flowers behind his back. Edwin grabbed his bow as two horses rounded the bend in the path, but he relaxed when he saw Adriana and her handmaid, Leena.

The young women reined in their horses, but Marcus only cared about Adriana. She jumped down before he could help her dismount.

"Sorry we're late. I had to convince Father not to send a guard with us."

"I'm just happy you made it. Two months with only letters is too long." He flicked a glance at Edwin. "Aren't you leaving?"

Edwin sighed and prodded his horse onto the path. "I'll be back in an hour or two."

Adriana leaned over, trying to peek behind Marcus. "What are you hiding?"

"A gift." He held the crown of red and pink wildflowers out to her. "When I saw them on the side of the road, I thought they would look even more beautiful in your hair."

A furrow formed between her eyebrows.

"You . . . made me a crown of flowers? Yourself?"

Heat suffused his cheeks as his hands drifted down. "I . . . I'm sorry. You're right. It's stupid. You probably have several real crowns—"

"No! I mean, I have a couple; it's just . . . I hadn't thought a prince would do such a thing." Adriana dipped into a small curtsy. "Will you put it on me?"

His heart in his throat, Marcus settled the crown atop her windblown chaos of blonde curls, then stepped back. For a moment, they stared at each other. Even though they were merely sixteen and he'd only known her since early autumn, he felt with a bone-deep certainty that one day, he would marry her.

But all he said was, "I was right. You make the flowers look as priceless as gems."

Adriana blushed. "I think it's my favorite crown."

The sky was an oppressive slate gray, the pasty oatmeal in his bowl flavorless, and Marcus's stocking had gotten twisted around uncomfortably in his shoe. Frigid air invaded the room through the open window with its single iron bar, but closing the wood shutters made the tower more depressing.

The small fire burning in the kitchen fireplace offered little light and less heat.

With a groan, Marcus slumped back in the stiff dining chair and stretched out his long legs. He raked a hand through his black hair, which was currently unbound, unbrushed, and falling around his shoulders in complete disarray.

Of course, there was no one there to see or care. Except for Edwin, who wouldn't judge him . . . much. Edwin sat across the table from him, eating his oatmeal and reading the same romance epic for at least the tenth time. His lengthy red-blond hair was already brushed and the top half neatly braided along the sides of his head and tied together at the back. Fastidious as ever, even though no one would see him, either.

Unless their monthly delivery of supplies arrived. It was late, again. That made four in a row. After the second time, they'd learned to ration the food, firewood, and water more carefully. Last time had been an entire two weeks late, and the supplies delivered had been less than usual and of lower quality. The servant and single accompanying guard had appeared skittish and worried. Of course, they wouldn't answer any of their questions. Everyone was, after all, under strict orders not to tell them anything of the world outside their prison.

Today would mark twelve days late for that month's delivery. Things were looking grim. They were down to one large wineskin of water and enough firewood for a few days at most—if they kept small fires going only when they were in the room, as they had been doing.

"Do you think he's forgotten about me?" Marcus asked, breaking the silence.

It was a question that had plagued him these past months, as the quality and frequency of their supplies declined, but one that, until then, he hadn't had the courage to voice.

Edwin looked up from his leather-bound book, but he didn't answer.

"My father," Marcus clarified. "Do you think he's forgetting about me, and keeps remembering too late to send the supplies, and one of these months, he'll forget entirely, and we'll starve?"

His mouth tightening, Edwin slipped a ribbon into the book and set it aside. "Truthfully? I've begun to wonder the same."

Some part of Marcus had hoped Edwin would offer reassurance, but that honesty was part of why Edwin was not only his servant but also his friend. Although, after almost four years stuck in the tower, Edwin was more like a brother.

"Or . . ." There was another possibility, one Marcus scarcely dared utter. "What if he finally got his war? And . . . he's losing?"

Edwin's solemn nod proclaimed he'd already arrived at the same possibility. "It would explain why the number of guards escorting the food dropped from four to one and why the condition and amount of food have fallen. Nothing more can be spared."

"And my father and brothers would have more pressing concerns than whether I starve." Marcus halfheartedly stirred the lumpy mash of oats before abandoning his spoon. Even if the food hadn't been awful, he no longer had an appetite.

"At least being locked up here means you haven't been called on to fight a war you never wanted to happen."

"A small consolation when neighbors might be dying on each other's swords right this moment for no reason other than the vanity of princes." He clenched his teeth and turned his attention to a barred window and the oppressive gray of the sky above the pines lining the edges of the valley.

A lesser gryphon flew over the treetops, too far away to make out what kind. Perhaps a hawk and bobcat variety. A few specks of white drifted into the valley, teasing the possibility of the first snowfall of the season. If Prince Arlius had gone to war, hopefully the fighting would end before winter began in earnest. A winter war would cause even more suffering . . .

No, it would be best if it was simply that his father had forgotten him. He didn't want to imagine how a war between the three regnant princes was harming the people of Aedyllan. Didn't want to wonder whether Adriana was spending her days waiting to hear if her father and brother had been killed in a battle for the kingship, as she'd always feared. He didn't like to worry whether the other kingdoms in Miraveld were watching Aedyllan tear itself apart and waiting to snatch up the pieces.

He'd once asked his father if fighting the other princes would make Aedyllan more susceptible to conquest, but his father dismissed the idea. Eynlae was too busy feuding with Rethalyon, Talland mostly kept to itself, and Kilkreth's current queen was focused on infrastructure. Marcus had begrudgingly admitted his father had a point, but that didn't mean war was a constructive proposition.

Sighing, he turned back to Edwin. "Either way, whether my father is busy with a war or he simply no longer cares, I'll make another attempt to escape before I lie down and die."

The words tasted hollow. There was no chance of escape.

Despite the fae spell placed on the tower, in that first month, they'd still attempted to break out, but the tower was impenetrable. The bars in the windows would not break or bend. The mortar between the stones could not be broken. The floorboards refused to budge to allow them to tunnel out, and attempting to break down the door was like fighting the side of a mountain.

"I'd expect nothing less of you." Edwin downed the last of his oatmeal, his expression serene, as if the coarse, bland food didn't bother him. "Practice sword bout after breakfast?"

Saying no and spending the day in listless sorrow was tempting but would ultimately make him more miserable—

almost certainly why Edwin had suggested a bout. He probably wouldn't take no for an answer, anyway. "Sure. How about a wrestling match to warm up?"

"I maintain that is not a normal way to warm up, but at least I usually beat you at wrestling, so, agreed."

As Edwin was a little bulkier, he was the better wrestler. His muscle-building regimen of exercises—and his novel-reading— kept him sane, while Marcus was more likely to run up and down the tower stairs to work out his excess energy. But Marcus had taught Edwin swordplay, and even with his extra lessons from the captain of the guard after he became Marcus's bodyguard, Edwin had never surpassed his first teacher.

A hollow boast for a confined prince who might never have occasion to put his swordsmanship to the test. Although he'd rather a practice fight with his friend in this forsaken tower than a blood-soaked blade on a battlefield strewn with the bodies of his own people.

"Ready now?"

Edwin eyed Marcus's half-eaten oats. "Finished already?"

"Oh, come on. It tastes like slush."

"Eating much muddy snow, are you? That seems unsanitary. Besides, there might not be more for a while." The corner of his mouth twitched. "Oats or slush, seeing as it has yet to snow."

The idea of throwing his oatmeal-covered spoon at Edwin

momentarily enticed Marcus, but then they'd have to clean up the mess and Edwin would insist on doing it and make him feel terrible, so he refrained.

"Then you eat it."

Edwin shook his head with a sigh and stood, scooping up both bowls. "I'll wash up. You go tame your hair or it's going to be a rat's nest after wrestling."

"Fine, fine."

While Edwin scraped the bowls clean and rinsed them using as little water as possible, Marcus lit the candle inside a metal lantern, then headed up the spiral stone staircase in the back corner.

Once upon a time, the tower had served as an important defense along some lord's border. That fief had been subsumed into a larger territory and the border moved, but the tower on its lofty, manmade hill in the middle of a valley had been maintained for emergency defense—until Prince Arlius had decided to turn it into a prison for his son.

The square tower consisted of four levels of one large room each, accessed by the spiral staircase inside the protruding stone attachment at the back corner of the tower. Thin arrowslits in the cylindrical outer wall of the stairwell illuminated the steep, narrow steps and small stone landings before the doors that opened to each level.

The ground floor held the kitchen, dining room, and a

small entrance foyer. They'd converted the second floor into a training area. Edwin had the third room to himself, and Marcus's bedroom was at the top. Or, almost the top—there was a crenelated roof, but the ladder to the roof hatch had been removed and the hatch barred and locked before their arrival. The roof had also resisted his efforts at escape.

There wasn't much to his bedroom. Three windows had wood shutters that, when closed, he could pretend didn't have iron bars on the other side. A desk and chair were placed beneath a window. A small bed with a feather-stuffed mattress covered in a pile of blankets rested on a wood frame that lacked posts and curtains. Another wood chair stood by the fireplace, and he had a chest full of clothes and a wood basin barely large enough to bathe in—although he'd had to give up baths and use only a wet rag since their supply deliveries had become unstable.

The used water, like his chamber pot, had to be hauled down to the first floor and dumped out a window that had only one bar and a chute to carry their waste to a pit dug at the base of the hill. Another window by the kitchen also had one bar, which allowed them to receive supplies, although it was a tedious process to pass sacks and crates back and forth through a window with a horizontal bar in the middle.

But Marcus would take the humiliation of pulling supplies through a prison window over starving to death. He had to live. Sooner or later, they would leave the tower. He refused to die without seeing Adriana again . . . even though sometimes he feared she hated him for disappearing without a word and wouldn't want to see him.

He glanced at his desk as he braided back the top half of his long hair. Two of the desk's four drawers were filled with letters to Adriana that he wasn't allowed to send. Then he'd run out of parchment and quills, and although Marcus had asked the servants to request more on his behalf, his father had never replenished them. Maybe the writing supplies and the small bookcase on the third floor full of common, well-worn books hadn't been left there intentionally as a kindness. Perhaps they'd merely been left by the previous occupant, and his father hadn't ordered them to be removed.

Marcus shook his head. There were many things he might never get answers to and wondering would only sour his mood further.

His cold fingers fumbled with his hair. At last, he had braided back the front section of his hair with two uneven plaits on both sides of his head, which he secured together at the back of his head with a thin strip of leather. The tails of the braids fell down over the rest of his loose hair. He jogged back down the steps, rubbing his icy hands. Edwin was already in the training room. He'd started the fire and was going through a series of defensive forms with one of the blunt training swords

Father had sent them toward the beginning of their stay—after months of Marcus sending messages back with the silent delivery servants.

On reflection, maybe his letters asking for the swords were why his father hadn't sent more writing supplies.

Edwin set aside his blunt sword and looked at Marcus with raised eyebrows. "After four years, you should be better at doing your own hair."

"It's not my fault there are no mirrors here. Not all of us can braid with our eyes closed."

"Mmm, but it's not *my* fault you refuse to let your servant do it for you."

"Servant where?" Marcus tapped his chin. "Wait, aren't you the prince's servant?" He faked a gasp. "But there's no prince here! So clearly, there's no servant, either."

Edwin kept his expression blank, but amusement showed in his eyes. "You were never officially stripped of your rank, Your Highness."

"That we know of." He strode onto the wool rug and began stretching to loosen up his muscles. "Besides, if I'm still a prince, you can't beat me at wrestling."

"Because you've always been such a rule-follower."

"I—"

A tremble shook the tower, and the words died on Marcus's lips.

CHAPTER 2

Pressed against Adriana in the wardrobe, gowns on either side forcing them close together, Marcus clapped a hand over Adriana's mouth to stifle her giggling. As much as their current situation amused him, it would be much less humorous if they were caught, especially by her father.

"Adriana?" Prince Mortimer Faine's footsteps made a dull clunk on the stone floor, then the rug muffled his steps as he walked in front of their hiding place.

She stiffened, and Marcus held his breath. While normally he'd rather be caught where he shouldn't be by Prince Mortimer than his own father, when he was alone in Adriana's bedroom—and a little bit tangled with her, squeezed as they were into the wardrobe—Prince Mortimer might not be forgiving.

Not that Marcus had done anything untoward.

But as his father had forbidden him from visiting the Faines, they concealed his presence from anyone who might mention him to Prince Arlius, which included Adriana's father. Since Marcus had sneaked into the castle, slipping in amid the chaos of a visiting noble family's departure, Prince Mortimer was unlikely to look upon their clandestine meeting favorably. A cowardly action, perhaps, but it was that or give up seeing Adriana entirely.

"Where has that girl gotten off to now?" her father muttered. He sighed, then his footsteps moved away, and the door closed.

Adriana pulled down on Marcus's hand, but he tightened his grip.

"Wait," he whispered.

They remained still for several more moments, until he was certain no one was in the room. He let out a breath, suddenly very aware of every place where their bodies touched as a result of cramming his tall frame into the wardrobe.

"Sorry." Sheepishly, he removed his hand from her mouth. "Needed to be sure the door closing wasn't a trick."

"Oh. I hadn't thought of that." Adriana pushed open the wardrobe doors, and Marcus squinted against the sunlight streaming in through her open window.

They both moved to get out at the same time. His foot caught on the hem of her dress, and they tumbled out of the closet. She half swallowed a scream and clutched the front of his long tunic, dragging him down despite his flailing efforts to catch himself.

His palms slammed painfully into the rug on either side of Adriana's blonde curls as he collapsed on top of her, and she released a muffled "Oooph." They both froze, their faces inches apart. His eyes locked with her hazel ones, and for a moment, he forgot to breathe.

Adriana's pink lips parted . . .

Heat crept into his face, and he scrambled off her. "Sorry." He brushed his long strands of dark hair over his shoulders, using the excuse of straightening his tunic over his legs to avoid looking at her. It was getting harder not to kiss her, but was eight months and fewer than a dozen meetings enough time to start kissing? Besides, he wasn't sure how to ask if she was interested in taking that step, too.

"Well." Adriana slipped around him on her

way back to the small table and motioned toward
the stacked deck of playing cards. "Shall we?"

Dust shook loose from the rafters as the tower quivered, and a low creaking, rumbling sound filled Marcus's ears. Edwin had gone white as a sheet, and he rushed over and seized Marcus's arm.

"We should . . . should . . ." Edwin's throat worked.

"You can't guard me from an earthquake." He'd meant it as a joke, but the words came out strained.

Then, as suddenly as it had started, the trembling ceased. The tower went still, as if nothing had happened. They stood frozen for several heartbeats, but no more tremors came, and the tower went silent. Marcus took a steadying breath, then pried Edwin's painful grip off his arm.

"I've heard stories about the earth shaking," Edwin whispered. "I wasn't entirely sure if they were true."

Marcus chewed on his lower lip. "I think it would be the first time here . . . but it seemed strange, somehow. Almost like the building itself was shuddering."

"That doesn't make sense."

"Does an earthquake make sense?"

They looked at each other, Edwin's troubled expression mirroring Marcus's confusion.

"Doesn't matter," Marcus said. "Regardless of the cause, it

might have affected the integrity of the tower."

"Meaning?"

Marcus grinned. "Meaning it might be weakened. We might have a chance to escape."

His eyes widening, Edwin looked around the room. "What do we try? The windows? The door?"

"Considering the bars are soldered into the stone, the door might be easiest and will quickly prove if the magic was affected or not."

Edwin nodded. "If the wood doesn't chip, we'll know nothing has changed."

After some debate about how to get started, Marcus attempted to pry the iron strap hinges off the door with a butter knife. When the knife wedged under the lower strap, he looked up at Edwin in stunned disbelief. Much straining later, they ripped the nails out of the wood and pulled away the lower hinge, leaving chips and scratches on the planks.

"The spell is gone," Edwin whispered.

Marcus nodded, still gaping at the bent hinge. After all these years, they could be free. He should be elated. Instead, dread crept through him.

"Do you think . . . my father . . ." He gulped. "He said until he orders the tower opened, or . . ."

Compassion softened Edwin's countenance. "Maybe he gave the order, and someone will be here soon. Or he might be testing you to see if you're strong enough to escape."

"Maybe." Marcus opened his mouth, about to ask if Adriana would be happy to see him again, but Edwin wouldn't know, either. Instead, he rose from his crouch and rolled his shoulders. "Back to work."

After they pried off the top hinge, they took turns digging out the nails and breaking apart the cracked and rotting horizontal planks. By evening the next day, they'd broken off the interior planks to reveal the outer, vertical layer of planks. These, unfortunately, proved difficult to separate from the plaster.

No one arrived to release them.

No one came with supplies.

Marcus threw himself into the demolition to avoid thinking about what they might face when they finally escaped.

Midmorning on the third day after the tower had quaked, they broke through the wood to the plaster itself. By midafternoon, frigid air whistled through a jagged hole.

When night fell, the opening in the door was almost big enough for them to fit through. Since leaving after dark in the freezing cold would be insane, and they were both exhausted anyway, they cooked some mushy root vegetables and went to sleep.

The following morning, Marcus's nervous excitement drove him to the door at dawn. By the time he'd knocked down sufficient plaster and wood to allow a comfortable exit, sweat pasted his tunic to his back despite the cold air. He dropped the battered training sword and leaned against the stone wall, closing his eyes as the wind whistled into the foyer.

"You're going to catch cold standing in that wind all wet," Edwin's disapproving voice said behind him.

Marcus snorted and shoved off the wall. "All right; I'll go change so you don't worry yourself to an early grave."

Edwin held out a couple pieces of stale, hard bread and a cup half filled with water. "Eat something first. Or I'll follow you around scowling."

"It's like having a particularly anxious nursemaid." But he forced himself to eat the barely edible food and wash it down with the water.

"That's the last of the food," Edwin murmured. "And the water."

Marcus froze. "Did you—"

"I'm fine."

"Ed—"

"We'll get something in town." He motioned at the door. "I'll be fine."

"I take it back. You're not a nursemaid. More like an insufferably self-sacrificial older brother." Marcus didn't have any experience with that kind of elder brother, but he'd read stories that claimed they existed. "Besides, as your liege, I am duty-bound to take care of my subjects, so I should have—"

"This is why I made you eat before I said anything." Edwin rolled his eyes. "You choose the most convenient times to change your mind about whether I'm your servant or your friend, and I don't like it when you give me orders that directly counter the solemn vows I made on the stars and Miraveld and my life to protect you."

The sacred oath of Aedyllan was part of a bodyguard's vows, and at the time, Marcus had been thrilled to have his man-servant and friend who had been by his side since they were both children double as his bodyguard. It had seemed much better than having some stranger following him around. Unfortunately, Edwin took those duties very seriously, and while Marcus appreciated his loyalty, it often made him feel awkward.

Marcus turned to the doorway. On the other side, dead brown grass stretched down the hill to the valley. The pines around the rim of the valley rose to meet the pale blue sky, and in the distance, a deer disappeared into the trees. An empty, unkempt road ran through the center of the valley and up to the tower. That road led to Alimer Castle, but first it passed through the closest town.

"I don't have a good plan for after we leave," Marcus admitted. "We don't have any coin, and if my father is . . . well, we might not have access to any money."

"No, but I'm sure we have some things we could trade for supplies, and we're both able-bodied young men who can exchange labor for food or shelter until we find a more permanent position."

Marcus kept staring out the door, his limbs heavy. Now that their escape was at hand, terror rooted his feet in place. What would they find? The aftermath of a war? Or that his father had forgotten him? Or perhaps that his father had grown tired of paying for his continued survival and had allowed him to escape merely to stop sending supplies?

Above all of those worries, another loomed.

What about Adriana?

Was she all right—healthy and happy and safe? Would she want to see him? Or would she have . . . moved on? He had clung to hope of escape for so long, had treasured the possibility of one day seeing Adriana again, of even wedding her. They had made each other promises. Still, years had passed. He'd never let the flame he carried for her flicker, but he'd had no other options. She would have had young men vying for her attention. She might not even know what had happened to him.

If he found her again only to discover she no longer cared for him, it might break him.

No, Adriana wasn't a fickle girl. Right? But then, he'd left first, even if he hadn't meant to. She had no proof he still loved her. Four years was enough time for someone else to have swept her off her feet. Marcus and Edwin might have been imprisoned for nothing.

Edwin cleared his throat. "Whatever happens, whatever we face out there, I have your back. You know that, right?"

His friend's words chased a little of the cold away from his heart. "Thank you." He turned toward the door, trying to suppress his worries, but his tongue developed a mind of its own. "Do you think she's forgotten me?" he burst out.

"Princess Adriana?" Edwin's forehead wrinkled. "If she had ever struck me as that capricious, I would have refused to help you sneak out and conceal your true whereabouts and wouldn't have delivered all those letters. And before you ask yet again, no, I still don't regret it. It's not our fault or Adriana's that your father is—" He abruptly cut off with a cough.

"Insane?" Marcus offered with a dry laugh.

Edwin shrugged. "Anyway. While you change, I'll finish packing. I've gathered clothes for both of us and anything of value, like the silver candlesticks."

"In what?" As far as he knew, they didn't have any packs.

"Sacks from our last food delivery. We can wrap blankets around the sacks and tie the blankets on our backs to fashion a sort of pack. Then we'll have blankets as well." He smiled ruefully. "I'm afraid we'll look more like vagabonds than a prince and his servant."

"Probably for the best, as we don't know what we'll face out there. Also, not a prince and servant."

Edwin just rolled his eyes.

Up in his room, Marcus found a clean change of clothes laid out on his bed. He shook his head, unsure what he'd done to deserve Edwin. He pulled on thick stockings, warm trousers, and a thin linen undertunic, then pulled on a gray outer tunic that came down to his shins. He ran his fingertips over the black embroidery on the collar. Well, he'd look like a formerly wealthy vagabond.

A fur-trimmed cloak, boots, and the only scarf and pair of gloves he had, and he was ready to go. He stilled, staring at the desk holding his letters for Adriana. Should he take them? Some of them he'd reread so many times when he had nothing else to do, he had them memorized.

Dear Adriana,

Remember when we first met? I couldn't sleep last night, and I kept thinking about how glad I am that I was the one who found you that day. It's selfish of me to be glad that you'd fallen from your horse onto a corroded riverbank and were clinging to an exposed root for dear life as the current pulled on your dress, selfish to be pleased that no one found you before me, but without that meeting, would we have grown close?

It's early autumn again, and from my bedroom window, I can see a hint of red maple leaves. I stare at them, and I'm back under that maple tree as the leaves fall around us. You're wrapped in my cloak in front of the fire I built, and I've pulled you close. I don't know you yet, I don't even know your name, but I think you're beautiful, and the chattering of your teeth and the way you shiver in my arms has me frightened—too frightened to leave your side to seek help.

You keep drifting off, but as long as you're still wet and cold, I won't let you sleep, afraid you won't wake back up. So I talk. I ramble on until you stop shaking and your hands are no longer frigid.

Do you remember the first thing you said to me?

"I hope you don't regret saving me, Prince Marcus."

I've never regretted saving you. Not when you told me who your father was—and I told you I didn't care; I'd attended his hunt because I dreamed of peace between our houses—not when my father scolded me for befriending you and forbade me from visiting or writing to you, not when I disobeyed him, not when I defied his order that I marry for his military alliance, and not now, trapped in this tower, do I regret saving you or falling in love with you.

I still have six and a half years left of my father's sentence, Adriana, but as soon as I'm free, I'll find you. The thought of holding you again gives me strength.

Please wait for me.

With all of my heart,

Marcus

Sighing, he turned away from the desk. Letters would take up precious space in their packs, and what would he do? Give her a stack of old letters and say, "Here, read these," when he could finally talk to her and hold her again? Assuming she even wanted that still. If things went poorly, end up using them as kindling and watching his dreams burn? Or worse, watch as Adriana herself tossed them into the fire because she no longer loved him? No, better to leave them behind.

Before leaving, he thoroughly smothered the fire. The tower could burn to the ground for all he cared, but if it did, the flames would likely take to the dry grass on the hill, from there to the valley and then the surrounding forests, and he refused to be responsible for burning down his people's lands. Once that was done, he picked up a candle and left his room at the top of the tower for the last time.

Edwin was waiting for him in the entrance hall. They helped each other tie on their makeshift packs.

"I've seen women carry their babes on their backs like this," Marcus complained.

"Would you prefer to carry it in your arms?"

"No, but that doesn't mean I like this."

"Then focus on the fact we're free and maybe that will lift your spirits." Edwin motioned toward the empty doorway. "Shall we?"

Marcus nodded. "I'm ready to never see this tower again."

CHAPTER 3

"Marcus? Hello? Marcus!"

Marcus blinked and Adriana's hand came into focus in front of his face, a miniature peach tart in her gloved fingers. Forcing a smile, he leaned forward and bit into the offered tart. The crust was perfectly flaky and the fruit delectable, but he scarcely enjoyed it.

"What's wrong?" She set aside the other half of the tart on the scratchy wool blanket they sat on and tucked a wild curl behind her ear. "Did something happen with your father?"

His shoulders slumped. "He's meeting with his counselors and general and my brothers more. More knights have moved into the castle, and he's been in contact with lords sworn to Prince Uldrich Nydellan. But Father and my brothers won't discuss what's happening with me, probably because I'd disapprove. I don't know . . ."

"What?" Adriana asked gently.

"Peace seems like a more futile dream every day. The things I most desire, I can't have."

She shifted to lean against him, and he wrapped an arm around her, adjusting his cloak so it protected both of them from the late autumn cold. "What do you desire?"

Marcus stared at the meadow full of grazing long-horned cattle, their long, shaggy red-brown hair stirring in the gentle breeze. Despite the chill, the sunlight warmed his face. Birds twittered nearby, and he caught the faint scent of rose in Adriana's hair. "This. This peace, for all of Aedyl-lan. And you, by my side forever, as my wife."

"Does 'this' include our own herd of fluffy cows?"

He mustered a smile. "As many fluffy cows as you require."

Adriana snuggled closer against his side. "I have to believe peace isn't a futile dream. If we can dream of peace, we can dream of us, too."

The nearest village was half a day's walk from the tower, and his father's castle was another half a day's walk beyond that. Clouds hid the sun, and the sky grew darker to the north, in the direction they were traveling. Rather odd-looking storm clouds for winter, but hopefully they'd make the village before the storm began. They pulled their scarves over their noses to thwart the cold wind that carried the occasional flurry of tiny ice crystals.

But the weather couldn't kill the bounce in Marcus's step as they walked through the center of the valley, then followed the road up the far end. Oh, how glorious it felt to stand below the open sky! How he'd missed dirt beneath his boots and the ability to walk more than a handful of steps before he reached a wall.

As they crested the side of the valley, Edwin pointed at the sky over the trees. "Those clouds . . . I have a terrible feeling."

Marcus eyed the drifting, foggy mass in the distance. They were heading right toward it, as if those clouds had gathered above Alimer Castle . . .

Over the castle.

He stumbled, his knees nearly giving out. "Edwin . . . what if it's not clouds? If it's—it's . . ." He gulped.

"Smoke."

After another hour of walking, they emerged from the trees into farmland, empty for the winter. The tip of Marcus's boot dragged through the muck as he stilled.

In the distance stood the stone and wood buildings of the village, but beyond them, a plume of dark smoke rose on the horizon.

One moment, Marcus was standing, the next he was on his knees in the thin layer of icy mud on the road, unsure how he'd gotten there. Edwin crouched beside him and laid a hand on his shoulder but didn't say anything. A tear burned its way down Marcus's cheek.

"My family is dead, aren't they?" he whispered. Deep down, he'd already known, but he hadn't been willing to admit it until faced with the truth.

Edwin's grip tightened on his shoulder.

The loss hurt more than he would have guessed. His father had always mocked him as weak-willed and had as good as abandoned him. His brothers hadn't saved him, and neither his father nor his brothers had so much as sent him a letter in four years. They hardly deserved the title of family. He hadn't been close with his aunt and uncle and younger cousins. Yet Marcus's chest squeezed as more tears slipped free.

His father and brothers had joined his mother in the afterlife.

He didn't know whether he was mourning the loss of their lives or the chance at reconciliation.

His childhood home was burning, or perhaps it had already burned and only the smoke remained. The action was likely a departing statement by whichever prince had won the war. In the end, his power-hungry, war-seeking father had brought about his own doom.

How many others had died or lost their homes? How many of the knights, courtiers, and servants at Alimer Castle had been killed? How many commoners across Alimer Principality had lost their lives to Prince Arlius's lust for power?

Maybe for all of those reasons, his father didn't deserve to be mourned. Perhaps Marcus's broken heart was as much anger as it was sorrow. Or maybe it was the weight of realizing that he was the only surviving member of his family.

He was alone.

No, not entirely alone.

Edwin still crouched at his side, his countenance somber as he offered quiet support. And perhaps Adriana—

Marcus jerked around and clutched Edwin's arm. "Adriana . . . do you think—if . . ." He shook his head, trying to clear his racing thoughts. "Did Uldrich and Mortimer join forces against my father? Or did they all fight each other? Is the war over, with one victor? And if only one prince is left . . . which one is it?" His fingers dug into the folds of Edwin's cloak. "What if it was Uldrich? What if he did this to Mortimer's castle, too, and Adriana is—"

"Easy, Your Highness. Slow down."

"Alimer Principality is overthrown." He released Edwin's arm and turned away. "I'm not a prince any longer."

Edwin stood with a sigh. "Our best course of action is to continue to town. We need supplies, and perhaps the residents will have heard whether Faine Principality stands."

Reluctantly, Marcus nodded and let Edwin help him to his feet. He frowned at the mud caking the front of his overtunic and trousers. Oh well. Maybe the mud would help him look less like a former prince.

"Considering we don't know the situation or the mood of the populace, I think we should keep my parentage secret." Marcus wasn't sure if he wanted to claim the association, anyway, after his father caused him and others so much hurt and suffering.

"Agreed," Edwin said. "So close to the castle and the tower, perhaps we should use false names."

Marcus set about coming up with their story so they wouldn't give conflicting answers. It helped distract him from the smoke on the horizon and what it meant.

By the time they reached the village around midafternoon, Marcus's stomach was gnawing at him. The town consisted of a mere dozen or so homes and a few shops near the central market plaza. A sign engraved with bread and a bed hung from an uneven building of plaster and wood, so they headed there.

Warm air from a roaring fire and the savory scent of food greeted them inside. Conversations fell silent as the few occupants of the inn's tavern looked over at them, eyes narrowed in suspicion.

A wiry woman with her graying brown hair pulled back in

a loose bun approached them, drying her hands on the apron about her waist. "Can I help you, sirs?"

"We're looking for some food and perhaps a place to stay for the night." Marcus shifted uncomfortably. "We don't have coin, but we have some valuables to trade."

She raised her eyebrows, looking them both up and down before shrugging. "What do you have?"

Edwin pulled off his makeshift pack and withdrew a silver candlestick.

The innkeeper leaned forward. "Tarnished, but is it solid silver?"

"Yes," Marcus said.

She held her hand out, and Edwin handed over the precious metal. A faint yellow shimmer glittered from her fingertips as she stroked the metal, her brow furrowed in concentration. Marcus stepped closer, fascinated. Alimer Castle's head cook had been an enchanter with a skill for herbs and food, but Marcus had never been allowed to watch him work.

Aedyllan had many enchanters compared to other kingdoms, although they still weren't common. Scholars suspected it was related to the unusually high fae activity within Aedyllan. It didn't particularly matter. Many enchanters had only a small amount of magic, and all suffered some kind of negative side effect from using it—most commonly fatigue, from what little Marcus knew about magic. Besides, few with the gift had the time or money to support the years of study and practice necessary to master their power, so some enchanters ignored their magic as mostly useless. Others pretended their magic didn't exist out of fear they'd be tempted by witchcraft, the casting of dark curses.

The candlestick gave a tiny shiver, and the tarnish fell from the metal in a fine dust.

With a satisfied smile, the innkeeper tapped a finger against her chin. "This will get ya both one meal an' one night in a shared room with other guests."

"We'll take it," Marcus said. He'd have preferred a private room, but he wasn't in the mood to haggle, and they needed to conserve their few valuables until they had a plan for the rest of their lives as commoners.

Planning for the rest of his life was hopelessly overwhelming, so he pushed that aside. One thing at a time, and for now, they needed food.

The innkeeper showed them to a small table in the corner with two chairs that creaked every time they moved. Nicks and gouges marked the worn surface of the tabletop, and when Marcus rested his forearm on the edge, the table wobbled. The only food on offer was a beef and vegetable stew with a slice of bread, which at least sounded decent. They settled back in their chairs as the innkeeper bustled away through a door in the back.

A man with streaks of silver through his long brown hair, which he wore out of his way in a topknot, shuffled over to their table. Dried mud splattered his trousers, short tunic, and the knobby cane he leaned on.

"You more of the king's men? Thought you'd all moved on."

Marcus started. "King?"

The man's brow scrunched. "Whaddya mean, 'king'? How could you have missed the news? It's posted in the marketplace." His gaze swept over them. "You don't look like men what ne'er learned to read."

They'd been too intent on food and in shock to even consider checking the marketplace for postings. Although he'd never had to learn news from a town crier or marketplace before.

He sat up and tilted toward the older man. "We've been in isolation for some time, as penance and for self-reflection."

Uncomfortably near the truth, but they'd needed a plausible reason why they wouldn't know the latest news. Spending a few years in a hermitage for spiritual reasons was likely to be too personal for anyone to ask prying questions.

"For how long?" The man shuffled out of the way as the innkeeper returned and placed food and tankards in front of them. "Helen, these boys don't know we got ourselves a king again."

The innkeeper whipped back around, loose tendrils of hair

flying about her face. "What's this? How?"

"Just came out of hermitage." The man shrugged.

"Well that won't do." Within moments, Helen had pulled up two more chairs, and she and the man with the cane settled on them.

Marcus experimentally sipped at the watery stew from a dinged pewter spoon and nearly melted into the chair. Herbs! They rarely had received seasoning beyond salt with their monthly supply deliveries, and even when they did, neither he nor Edwin had had the slightest notion how to use them appropriately.

"It all started about . . . oh, two years ago," Helen said, her expression lighting up like she relished the opportunity to tell the story. "Some nobles in Nydellan Principality stirred up a revolt against Prince Uldrich, and there were rumors Prince Arlius was involved, so Prince Uldrich asked Prince Mortimer for aid—wait, you do know who the three princes were, right?"

His mouth full of savory carrots and broth, Marcus nodded.

"Well, after they put down the revolt together, Prince Uldrich got the idea that Prince Mortimer would be easy pickin's while his army was still in Nydellan Principality."

The man tsked. "Fool. Prince Mortimer wiped out the entire Nydellan family and claimed the lands for himself."

"Aye, so then Faine Principality was two-thirds of Aedyllan," Helen said. "Prince Arlius didn't appreciate that and invaded Faine Principality while Prince Mortimer was still on his way home. Probably thought Faine Castle would be defenseless and Faine's army exhausted."

Marcus winced. Of all the foolish, underhanded, and cowardly things to do . . . no wonder Prince Mortimer had razed Alimer Castle.

"Did him no good," interjected the old man. "Prince Mortimer brought men from his expanded principality and had left plenty of knights to guard his family. He drove Prince Arlius back to his own castle."

"You probably saw the smoke." Helen shook her head. "Arlius was killed four days ago, and the next day, Mortimer was crowned in Alimer Castle. Then he had it burned. It's been three days, but it's still smolderin'."

"Prince Mortimer claimed the title of King of Aedyllan and had it announced all over the kingdom," the man said. "Course, there's also the rumors."

"Rumors?" Marcus asked.

The man nodded gravely. "There's word about that Mortimer Faine isn't king now by mere skill alone." He leaned in, his tone conspiratorial. "Some say he was aided by the fair folk."

CHAPTER 4

Prince Mortimer scowled, his arms crossed over his chest, revealing bulging muscles even through the long sleeves of his ankle-length tunic. "Prince Marcus Alimer, you say? Why in Aedyllan do you wish to see my daughter?"

"I was the one who found her during the autumn hunt, Your Highness." Marcus gulped. They had met at that time, but Mortimer had been too worried about Adriana to spare Marcus more than a passing glance.

"Oh. Thank you." The intimidating prince eyed him, and Marcus had the sinking feeling he didn't measure up in some way. Perhaps it was a good thing Adriana's father didn't know about the letters they'd exchanged over the last three weeks. "How old are you?"

"Sixteen." His voice cracked, because of course his body would choose that moment to betray him.

Adriana's father snorted. "You seem innocent and foolish enough that you likely aren't a threat. Besides, I've heard the rumors that you don't get along with your father, so I suppose he didn't send you for some nefarious purpose." He shrugged and stepped out of the doorway, motioning Marcus into a narrow hall. "I'll send for her. She'll want to thank you in person, as is proper."

When Adriana entered the hallway several minutes later, a gold circlet tucked into her blonde curls and a violet dress swishing about her legs, Marcus finally understood why people described beauty as enchanting. Because when she smiled, he could have sworn she'd cast a spell on his heart.

"Fae?" An unpleasant sensation twisted in Marcus's gut. Would Mortimer do something as risky as dealing with the fae? Sure, Marcus's own father had used a fae curse to keep him trapped in a tower, but Mortimer had always seemed more astute.

"Aye," Helen said. "There's two stories circulatin'—first that Mortimer found his way into the fae realm and asked to rule Aedyllan, and the other—"

"That he rescued a fae lass, and she granted him a boon," the man cut in.

"Owen, am I tellin' this story or you?"

"Thought we both were."

She rolled her eyes. "Anyway. I like the story that he saved a lady's life, not knowing she was fae, so she granted him a wish."

"Either way," Owen said with an irritated frown, "I heard from a man who heard it from a knight who heard it from Prince Jairus Faine himself that a fae blessed the Faines to rule Aedyllan for all time. Though some say there's some curse or prophecy that says their reign will end if somethin' specific happens, but I say if that were true, the king wouldn't let a soul know about it. But everybody says the Faines are fae-blessed now."

Did the fae actually possess *that* much power? That was sobering. If this story was true, when had it occurred? Perhaps if Arlius Alimer had known, he would have been motivated to pursue peace with Mortimer instead of causing his own death. Although a man secure in a fae blessing that he would rule a kingdom might not be easy to reason with. It was also possible Arlius *had* heard and attacked out of fear.

"What of the rest of the Alimer family?" Edwin asked quietly, speaking the question Marcus couldn't bring himself to utter. "Prince Arlius's sons and sister and nieces and nephew?"

"All dead," Helen declared with ringing finality that pricked at Marcus's weary heart. "How could Mortimer declare himself king otherwise?"

"Well, 'cept mayhap the youngest princeling." Owen shrugged. "But reckon he'll starve in that cursed tower without supplies."

"Be what he deserves, the coward," Helen spat.

Marcus fumbled his spoon, almost dropping it. He forced down a bite of bread that had turned to clay in his mouth. "What's this?"

"Oh, you've been away that long?" Owen whistled. "About . . . oh, four years ago, now, Prince Arlius locked his youngest son in a tower in the valley near here for refusing an arranged marriage."

Helen sniffed. "Some folks thought the truth was that Prince Marcus didn't agree with whatever trouble his father was stirring up in Nydellan; others said he wanted to make peace with Faine. But you know what I think? He was a coward who claimed peace but did nothin', and as a result, he spent this war safe in a tower away from all the fightin' and dyin'.

"You tell me"—she jabbed a finger toward Marcus—"if you were the prince and you'd known the Alimers were inciting a rebellion in Nydellan, and you really wanted peace, wouldn't you warn Prince Uldrich? Or alert Prince Mortimer? Or agree to the marriage but leverage the union for peace? If Prince Marcus opposed what his father was doing, why'd he let himself get locked up in a tower to be useless? If his goal was peace, like some folks said, he did a miserable job of it."

Owen scratched his chin. "Not sure if he could'a stopped it, though. Those princes had been movin' toward war for a decade or more. Far's I've heard, that young prince was the only one what ever wanted to cooperate with the other princes, rather than covetin' a throne."

"Bah." Helen pushed to her feet. "I think he feared war more than he wanted peace, so he chose a tower over a marriage." With a dismissive wave, she headed back to the kitchen.

Cold crept over Marcus. He stuck his spoon in his bowl, leaving the last few bites of soup and bread, and leaned back, his appetite gone. How many times had he wondered if he should do something more, only to convince himself that it wouldn't have worked . . .

A memory forced its way into his consciousness. He was sixteen, and he'd just returned from Prince Mortimer's autumn hunt, where he'd met Adriana—and where he hadn't been supposed to go.

"Fool of a boy! I told you we weren't going!" His father's face turned red from the force of his shouting.

Marcus slouched further into his chair at the head table in the great hall, wishing his hair wasn't braided so he could let it fall over his face and hide him from the entire castle's residents currently assembled for dinner—and all staring at him.

He drew a steadying breath. "I thought—"

"Are you trying to undermine me?" his father demanded.

"Betray me to Faine?"

"N-no!"

His eldest brother, Fabian, snorted. "As if he's either clever or brave enough for that."

"I just want peace," Marcus whispered.

"What was that?" His father leaned around his second eldest son as he glared at Marcus. "Speak up!"

"Something about peace," Linus scoffed. "Why should we want peace, then, Marcus? Wouldn't uniting Aedyllan under Father as king bring peace? What's so great about the Faines since you've been consorting with them?" As Father settled back into his own chair, Linus swept his hand out at the crowd. "You have a captive audience. Convince us."

Heat flamed over Marcus's face, and his throat closed up. What could he say? That he'd befriended Princess Adriana, and she seemed like a good person? That Mortimer cared about his family and therefore must be good, too? No, this was his chance to make a point of how a war would hurt Aedyllan and cause so much unnecessary death for so little gain. He could talk about his idea of strengthening relationships between the principalities so they could work together instead of hindering each other's efforts. But his tongue seemed to have turned to lead.

What was the point? Father was already angry, so he wouldn't listen. Most likely no one else would be convinced, *either. His brothers would torment him for daring to voice such "foolishness." Things would only get worse. Father might forbid him from leaving the castle, and then he couldn't try to visit Adriana. Although he'd probably have to put that off for a while, so Father wouldn't get suspicious, anyway.*

Fabian snickered. "It seems he's forgotten how to speak."

"Naturally," Father muttered. "Then do what you're best at, child. Stay silent and stay out of my way."

And he had, more often than not. Sneaking about, trying not to draw attention to himself, hiding his relationship with Adriana, lying that he would stop seeing her when his father confronted him with the truth. He'd complain but not put up a fight when his father left him out of counsel meetings, and any time he did speak up, he'd retreat at the first hint of pushback, convincing himself that there'd be a better opportunity in the future.

He'd thought he was strategically waiting until he had a plan or knew the right words, or the perfect time presented itself. Eventually the tensions between the princes would lessen, he'd tell himself, providing an opportunity to make his argument. After all, if he acted too soon or his arguments were too weak, he'd make things worse, right?

He hadn't tried to marry Adriana for the same reason. Sure, they'd promised each other they'd get married, but it was always *someday.* He'd avoided the question of *when* and dodged her suggestion that they elope. Even Edwin had said that was foolish, providing a litany of reasons why it wouldn't work and might cause more conflict, and Marcus had been quick to accept them.

Should he have done more than wish and dream and hazard on occasion to voice his dissent to his father and brothers? It was true that he hadn't run away or revealed his father's plotting and had neglected chances to speak up or act because he'd feared repercussions. What if, had he been more decisive despite the potential danger to himself, he could have prevented the war?

Not yet had subconsciously become his motto back then. *It's not the right time yet. I can't do anything. Better to wait for now. Things will get better, and I'll figure out what to do then . . .*

Deep down, he knew he'd been avoiding conflict and hiding from the chance of failure.

Maybe that did make him a coward.

Marcus hadn't felt like a prince in years, but maybe he'd never behaved like one at all.

Edwin caught his eye from across the table, his expression sympathetic as he gave a small shake of his head.

"Well, I've got to see the herbalist before he closes up for the day." Owen stood with a muffled groan, then lightly tapped the cane against his right leg. "Deep cut during the fighting that was stitched poorly. Trying to get it back to rights again." He winked. "Which I wouldn't have told ya if you'd been the king's men. But no point holdin' malice, says I. War's over, and Prince Arlius got what he sowed. This pain's more his fault than King Mortimer's."

With that, the man shuffled out of the inn.

After a few moments of silence, Edwin leaned over the table. "It's not true," he whispered.

Marcus sighed and jabbed his finger into the remaining bit of bread. "No, he's right," he said quietly. "My father brought this to himself and on his own people. I didn't make those choices for him."

"I meant what the innkeeper said. It's not your fault."

"Maybe she's right, too." He dropped the bread into the bowl. "I could have done more. I—"

"Does it matter?" Edwin interrupted. "You can't change the past. Perhaps you can learn from it, but you can't change it—no amount of dwelling on it or thinking of alternatives will allow you to do anything differently. Perhaps nothing you could have done would have avoided this outcome. But what you *did* do had one positive result for certain: you're still alive. That means you're free to be more decisive in the future if you so choose, but don't use your survival to wallow in guilt over an alternate path that you don't know the outcome of and can't take anyway."

Gaping at his friend, Marcus slumped back and chuckled. "That's rather philosophical and wise of you." It was also difficult for Marcus to accept, even if he agreed.

Edwin lifted a shoulder. "Four years is a lot of time for self-reflection, and I quickly realized it was also plenty of time for me to wonder if I regretted helping you and getting myself thrown in that tower. I don't," he added as guilt pricked at Marcus, "so don't beat yourself up over that, either. You tried to speak up for me, and I'd known what I was doing. But more than a simple question of regret or not, I realized dwelling on the past wouldn't help."

"Well now I feel self-conscious that you used our forced isolation to better your mind and spirit as if we were, in fact, in a hermitage for self-improvement."

"As if you haven't become more contemplative yourself and somehow kept hope this entire time, to say nothing of being so quick to question if you could have done something more instead of shrugging it off without a moment of self-reflection.

"Actually, at times . . . I've envied you." Edwin tugged on a lock of red-blond hair. "Most of the time over these last few years, you've been focused on the future and held so much hope. Some days I was trying to just get through the day without losing my mind, and then you'd say something about *when* we get out. Sometimes I couldn't understand how you were so sure, and yet"—he spread his hands—"here we are."

"Oh." Marcus bit the inside of his lip. "I'm sorry . . . I didn't realize you were struggling, too. I should have noticed." He pulled the tankard of weak ale to the edge of the table. "Maybe I should have been honest with you on the days I felt like I was running out of hope and sanity. But I didn't want to look like I couldn't handle it . . . not when you always seemed so calm and put-together in spite of everything. So I faked optimism even when I didn't feel it."

They stared at each other for a minute before they both laughed. Shaking his head, Marcus finished off his ale.

"Well," Edwin said drily, "seems four years wasn't sufficient to teach us to be honest."

"We'll figure it out going forward, I'm sure." Marcus's smile faded. "Except . . ." How was he supposed to ask if they'd be going forward together? "My family is gone. My crown is gone and so is any income, and any way of paying you."

"So I'm not your servant or bodyguard anymore."

"You haven't been that to me for a long time. But I don't expect you to stay—"

"Nonsense." Edwin waved a hand. "What else am I supposed to do? You know my parents died when I was young. It's not as if you'll hold me back or something. I haven't had to look for work before, either. We might as well muddle through this together. At least we'll have each other."

A relieved smile pulled at Marcus's mouth. "Yes. Muddling through this together sounds easier."

"Any idea what you want to do?"

He rubbed his thumb over an indent in the tabletop. "Perhaps it's foolish, but first, I'd like to go to Faine Principality. Although, I suppose that isn't what it's called anymore. No more co-regnant princes, no more principalities . . . But I'd like to get word of Adriana. Make sure she's all right. Perhaps attempt to let her know I'm alive."

Edwin frowned. "Is that safe? Her father just . . . you know."

"Wiped out my entire family?"

"Yes."

Marcus pushed his fingernail along a groove in the wood table. Avoiding Faine Principality would be safer, both for his life and his heart. He could wait for word to reach him instead of searching it out, wait until there was some indication of whether Mortimer would be lenient with the son of his former rival and whether Adriana was still waiting for him . . . but if he was going to learn from his past mistakes, didn't that mean he should stop holding back out of fear? Besides, going to Faine Principality meant less time spent wondering about Adriana and manufacturing worst case scenarios.

He took a deep breath. "I'm sorry. I need to know she's all right."

After a moment, Edwin nodded. "I'm not surprised. At

least that gives us a destination. We can determine what to do next when it's time."

"Thank you, Ed. For everything." He didn't know how to properly put into words how much it all meant to him—how Edwin hadn't grown bitter over the last four years, had offered quiet support through all of the revelations of the day, and had understood that Marcus couldn't rest until he knew that Adriana was all right.

Just then, the front entrance opened. A man stalked in, his face hidden under the black cowl of his cloak. White flecks of snow melted on his clothing. A sword hung at his side and two daggers glinted on the baldric across his chest. The innkeeper scurried out of the back.

"Can I help you, sir?"

The newcomer tossed back his hood, revealing long brown hair braided away from his forehead and a tanned, hawkish face with sharp eyes. "Do you have accommodations for the night?"

"Aye."

He nodded and reached under his cloak, withdrawing a large sack of clinking coins. "How much for my own room?"

"A gold piece."

"And for information?"

She tilted her head. "Depends on the information."

"I'm looking for Prince Marcus Alimer."

CHAPTER 5

"It scares me to death every time you climb that trellis."

"What scares me is the thought that one day I could arrive, and it will be gone, torn down to keep me out."

Adriana rolled her eyes, a teasing smile playing about her mouth. "I say I'm worried about you falling to your death, and you're only worried about how you'll get in?"

Marcus didn't smile. "If the trellis was gone, that'd mean your father found out about us and is preventing me from seeing you. I think a part of me would die if I could never see you again, Adriana."

Her grin faded as she stared at him. "Marcus . . . If things keep going the way they are . . . you said yourself you suspect your father is stirring up trouble in Nydellan Principality. We don't know what could happen. If a conflict does arise, you might not be able to sneak out." She stepped closer and placed her soft hand against his cheek. "If that happens, we won't give up on each other, will we?"

The fervency in her eyes ignited a similar resolve within him. "Of course not. No matter how difficult things get or how far apart we are, we'll keep hope that we'll see each other again, no matter how long it takes."

Marcus spun away from the door and ducked down in his chair. With a frown, Edwin leaned closer and spoke so quietly Marcus almost couldn't hear him, "You look suspicious."

"Oh, that's so easy it's free," Helen exclaimed. "Prince Marcus has been in a tower in the valley just south of here for years. You're on the right track, but you're also right you'll be needin' a place to stay tonight. No sense travelin' in the dead of night, and sun's already settin'."

"He's still in the tower?" the man covered in blades asked.

"Far as we know. King Mortimer send you to release him?"

The man was silent for a moment. "Something like that."

Marcus blanched. *Assassin?* he mouthed.

By Edwin's grim look, he had concluded the same thing.

Helen led the man upstairs, and Marcus tried to calm his mounting panic.

"He likely doesn't know what you look like," Edwin whispered. "So if we don't do anything to give ourselves away, we'll be fine. He'll go to the tower in the morning, and we'll head toward Faine Castle, and he'll never find you."

If only Marcus shared that surety.

But it was so much worse than simply avoiding his own death.

If that man truly had been sent by Mortimer Faine to kill him . . . visiting Adriana would be even more dangerous. Sure, Mortimer likely wouldn't recognize him, as they hadn't seen each other in roughly five years and they'd only met each other twice, and one of those times Mortimer had been distracted with other concerns. But it would still be insanity to go near Faine Castle if Mortimer wanted him dead.

He scowled at his cold remaining stew. Did the new king fear the son of one of his vanquished rivals might pose a threat to his nascent reign? Understandable, but that couldn't be further from the truth. Marcus had never cared about ruling, and even if the route had been one he'd hoped to avoid, Mortimer *had* brought peace to Aedyllan, which was all Marcus had ever wanted.

Other than Adriana.

Without a crown and now that Adriana was the princess of an entire kingdom, he'd already known he didn't have a chance anymore. He was hardly a suitable husband, and he had no wealth or plan to provide for her if they eloped. Still, in the deepest part of his heart, he'd clung to the hope that they could be together. After all, Adriana wasn't the heir, that was her older brother, so there was a possibility her father wouldn't care who she married, as long as he was a good man.

But if Mortimer Faine wanted him dead, would he ever accept Marcus as his son-in-law? Perhaps if he convinced Mortimer he wasn't a threat. He could establish contact with Adriana and wait until Aedyllan had stabilized, then reveal himself and prove he'd done nothing to undermine the new king. He'd already waited four years. What was another several months?

Of course, none of this would matter if Adriana didn't even want him anymore. If only he knew for certain she was waiting for him, but the only way to know that was to go to her—or at the very least, to the town near her father's castle. He had to know.

"Unless . . ." Edwin said quietly, interrupting his thoughts. "Are you sure you still want to go to Faine Castle?"

Oh, he knew he shouldn't. It was foolish beyond measure. "Yes." His heart wouldn't let him give any other answer.

Edwin's lips thinned in a way that indicated he didn't approve, but that he wouldn't argue, either.

When Helen came back down the stairs, Marcus asked her to show them to their accommodations.

She escorted them upstairs, past a couple of closed doors and some that were open to small rooms with one or two beds, to the end of the hall. A curtain hung over the doorway, which she pushed aside before motioning for them to follow. She pulled flint and steel from a pocket of her apron and lit a candle on a sconce mounted to the wall. Feeble light illuminated a room with six beds that were little more than cots, but it looked clean and didn't smell, so Marcus decided it wasn't bad.

"That bed's taken." The innkeeper indicated a cot on the right side of the room. "But you have your pick of the others. If you need to leave the room, just turn the top half of the blanket down the same as that one to show that bed's claimed. You can light any of the candles"—she motioned to the handful of other candles on the walls—"but blow them out if you're leaving the room empty."

"Thank you." Marcus narrowly stopped himself from bowing. No need to betray his noble upbringing, especially with a dangerous stranger lurking nearby who was looking for him.

Helen grunted and departed. Edwin looked around the room with a scowl.

"What? It's better than I'd pictured."

"Only one exit, unless we count the window," Edwin muttered. He pointed to where a cowhide had been affixed to the left, west-facing wall, likely covering a window for the winter. "Which, considering how far we'd fall from there, I don't. If that assassin comes for you in here, we'll be trapped, and with no door, we can't even lock him out."

"I thought you said we didn't need to worry."

"There's a difference between worrying and being cautious."

"Is there?"

Edwin made a face at him. "I suppose there's nothing to be done for it. It'd attract suspicion if we asked for our own room now, and I'm not sleeping outside."

"Nothing other than sleep is going to happen," Marcus said, and he hoped he sounded unworried.

Still, Edwin insisted they take the two cots under the window, despite Marcus's protests about the cold air seeping in around the wood shutters and hide covering. "It's further from the unknown person sharing the room, and I can indulge my fantasy that the window is a means of escape in an emergency."

They spent the rest of the evening discussing the best route to reach Faine Castle, until a quiet young man arrived and tucked into the cot on the far side of the room. Thankfully, they'd made enough secret excursions to meet with Adriana that they were well acquainted with several possible routes.

It took a while for Marcus to fall asleep. Thank goodness for the blanket that Edwin had used to tie on his pack, because the inn's blankets were scratchy. The thin, straw-stuffed mattresses were lumpy and uncomfortable, but were better than sleeping on the ground. Quiet snoring came from the far end of the room. And in the back of his mind, the likely assassin somewhere down the hall taunted him every time he closed his eyes.

Somehow, though, he did sleep, and when he awoke, it was to find Edwin already up and stretching beside his bed in the flickering light of a single candle. Of course his red-blond hair was already brushed and re-braided, too.

Well, he probably slept better, Marcus thought irritably.

Their roommate was still lightly snoring, but Marcus caught a faint scent of baking bread, so he might as well get up.

After Marcus cleaned up and found the water closet, they repacked their things and headed downstairs. A door opened as they passed it, and the man in the black hood from the night before emerged. They gave each other a silent nod and Marcus and Edwin hurried past, Marcus acutely aware of the man walking behind them.

No one else was in the dining area downstairs, but a middle-aged man with his long hair tied back at the nape of his neck and a ruddy complexion entered from the kitchen.

"Oh, sirs! Are you lookin' to break your fast?"

"Yes." A chill went through Marcus as he and the man hunting him spoke at the same time.

"If it can be quick," the assassin said as he stepped around Edwin. "A couple of fried eggs should do it. I need to be on the road, and I'll pay extra to be on my way faster."

"Ah, somewhere important to be?"

"I need to find the young Alimer princeling, and I've heard a theory the curse making his prison inescapable may have broken with his father's death." The man slipped into a chair, his movements smooth as a bobcat's. "Seen anyone unusual pass through in the last few days?"

Marcus and Edwin took a table on the opposite side of the room. If it weren't for hunger already gnawing at his stomach, he would be tempted to leave without breakfast.

The ruddy-faced man laughed. "Sure. You, them over there"—he jerked his thumb toward Edwin and Marcus, and Marcus resisted the urge to flinch—"think there's another 'un upstairs. And a host of knights and soldiers in the last week."

"I see. The eggs, if you would?" The assassin flipped a gold coin between his fingers. "And a loaf of bread, if you have it."

"Aye." A greedy glint shone in the innkeeper's eyes as he turned to Marcus and Edwin. "And for you, sirs?"

Edwin held out a brass candle snuffer with an ivory handle. "Whatever we can get in exchange for this. If it'd cover something for us to take on our way, that would be appreciated."

The man examined the snuffer before nodding. "Be right out." Then he disappeared into the back.

Marcus glanced toward the cloaked man and wished he hadn't when he caught the assassin watching them. He focused on Edwin.

"What do you suppose he'll bring us?"

"Eggs, probably. Fast and cheap. Beyond that, I have no idea."

Steady bootsteps moved toward them, then a scraping of wood against wood, and the assassin dragged a chair over to their table. "What's your story?"

Marcus braced himself as he turned and met the man's gaze and worked to keep his expression neutral. "Just passing through on our way home."

"I'm Darius." He tilted his head, clearly waiting for them to give their names.

"Gerald," Marcus said evenly. "This is my brother, Felix."

Darius nodded. "Did you fall on hard times as a result of Prince Alimer's defeat?"

"No. Recently came out of seclusion for spiritual betterment."

"Truly?" Darius lifted his eyebrows, his gaze passing up and down them both. "Where's home?"

"Nydellan Principality. Or what used to be Nydellan." Marcus's hands grew clammy, and his appetite was quickly fading.

"Must be strange to come out of seclusion and find so much changed." Something in the man's piercing eyes made Marcus's mouth go dry.

"Indeed. We worry about how our family is faring."

The door to the kitchen swung open, and the male innkeeper breezed out, three plates balanced on his arms and a sack in each hand.

"Here—ah, makin' new friends? Excellent." He placed all three plates of eggs on their table, much to Marcus's chagrin. "And bread for the road." He gave a sack to Edwin and exchanged the other for a gold coin from Darius before striding back to the kitchen.

"Why are you looking for this princeling?" Edwin asked, his tone almost too casual as he cut into his eggs.

Darius picked up his own butterknife and fork. "I've been sent to kill him."

CHAPTER 6

Marcus barely managed not to stab himself in the mouth with his fork as his hand jolted.

"So you casually admit to murder?" Edwin asked.

The assassin shrugged. "Is it murder if the king commands it or merely a private execution?"

"For what crime?" Marcus demanded, immediately wishing he hadn't said anything. "I understand this prince has been imprisoned for years. How could he have wronged our new king while behind bars?"

Darius swallowed a large bite of eggs. "Existing? The king dislikes loose threads, I suppose. It's my job to do my king's bidding, not to ask questions." He met Marcus's gaze. "Why do you care, Gerald?"

Marcus focused on the remaining egg on his plate. "I'd like to think now that Aedyllan has a king again at last, he will be a just one."

"What I don't understand," Edwin said, "is why now? I heard Prince Arlius was killed five days ago. Why only now?"

"As I said, not my place to ask questions." The assassin took another large bite before adding, "Perhaps he forgot. He returned to his own castle, and then the next day, he sent me to take care of the last Alimer."

The furrow between Edwin's eyebrows mirrored Marcus's confusion. Had Adriana asked about him, and that had prompted her father to send an assassin after him? A worse thought churned his stomach. Or did she hate him so much for disappearing without a word that she also wanted him dead? No, Adriana would never do that, not intentionally.

Darius finished his eggs and stood. "Well. It was a pleasure conversing with you, Marcus."

Absently, Marcus grunted, then froze. "I'm—it's Gerald."

But it was too late.

As Darius drew a knife with a wicked grin, Edwin flipped the table over on its side. Grabbing a fistful of Marcus's tunic, Edwin yanked him behind the makeshift barrier so quickly, Marcus nearly slammed his head against the single support in the middle of the table.

"Don't be foolish, princeling." Darius chuckled. "You can't escape, and you aren't armed. If you come out now, I'll make it quick."

Marcus gritted his teeth. He hadn't escaped the tower alive to die in an inn before he even found out if Adriana was all right. Still, tables and chairs and perhaps the utensils scattered out of reach made poor weapons against knives and a sword. He peered around the edge of the table at the front door, far across the room and with the assassin blocking the way.

"The kitchen," Edwin whispered. "There must be a back entrance. On three, run."

Despite wanting to argue or demand to know the plan, Marcus nodded. They didn't have time for discussion, and he trusted Edwin.

"One . . . two . . . three."

Marcus sprang up while Edwin grabbed the table leg and shoved the table toward the assassin. As Marcus sprinted toward the kitchen, the male innkeeper emerged, a large rolling pin in hand.

"What's this racket—oy!" The innkeeper broke into a run. "What're ya doin', pullin' weapons in my inn?"

"Marcus!" Edwin cried out, just as something flashed in the corner of Marcus's vision.

Marcus turned, and his eyes widened as a knife flew through the air directly toward his chest. He dove to the side, but not fast enough. The knife grazed his temple, and a fiery pain blossomed near his left eyebrow. Momentarily stunned, he fell and the side of his head slammed into the wood floor.

The dining room blurred as a throb hammered his skull. He moaned and tried to get up. The last thing he saw before passing out was Edwin shoving a chair into Darius while the innkeeper cracked the rolling pin against the assassin's head.

Marcus jolted awake and immediately regretted the movement as his aching head spun. Something sticky pulled at his left eye, and he wiped at something tacky and wet. Forcing his eyes open, he gaped down at the blood smeared over his hand.

"You're awake." Crouching next to him, Edwin slumped in relief, then cast a nervous glance to the side.

His mind cleared and his surroundings came back into focus. Marcus sat on the dirt, slumped against an exterior wall. Warm air crept out of the open door to his left.

"How long was I unconscious?"

"Not long. You woke up for a few moments as I was dragging you through the kitchen, then passed out again briefly." Edwin stood and offered his hand. "We need to get moving. I doubt that assassin will be out long, either."

Marcus accepted Edwin's help to get to his feet. The world tilted and spots danced in Marcus's vision for a moment. He wiped more blood away from his eye. "Need to stitch that cut," he mumbled.

"Soon," Edwin agreed as he gripped Marcus's arm and led him away. "The innkeeper confiscated the assassin's weapons and was tying him up while I was pulling you out. He was furious about the blood all over his floor, but once the assassin wakes up and explains he's on a mission from the king, the innkeeper will probably let him go."

They hurried toward a barn and stables standing in the field behind the inn. Beyond that rose the forest, but Marcus didn't think he could make it that far, and Edwin's course seemed to head directly for the barn.

"I don't want to steal a horse."

"Of course you don't." Edwin didn't slow. "I'm hoping there's a place to hide."

Marcus squeezed his eyes shut, the cloudy sunlight too bright. His aching head felt weighed down by lead, and every step sent another jarring burst of agony through his skull. The pack on his back threatened to send him off-balance, and he leaned against Edwin's shoulder to steady himself.

It was agony, but they made it into the barn. Bales of hay were stacked along one wall, a chicken coop filled the other, and two cows were tied along the third wall. Various crates and sacks were stacked around the remaining wall.

The clucking of the chickens pressed against Marcus, intensifying the throbbing in his head. They tucked themselves into a space between a pile of crates and the barn wall that was just wide enough for them to sit down.

After making a makeshift binding for Marcus's wound using his scarf—which left Marcus's left eye partly covered— Edwin guided his hand to press against his wound.

"Keep pressure on that. Don't lie down. I'm going to peek

out to see what's happening. Don't move from this spot."

Before Marcus could answer, Edwin jogged away. A moment later, the barn door creaked, then latched shut again. Had he left the barn entirely? What was he up to?

The minutes dragged on, each one longer than the last. Marcus curled against the wall with his eyes closed, his head angled to keep pressure on the cut. What if Darius had hurt Edwin, or worse? What was taking him so long? He considered going to look for him, but when he moved, a wave of nausea hit him, and the pounding in his skull came roaring back.

After what seemed an eternity, Marcus could no longer wait. His nerves had frayed to the point of snapping. He couldn't lose Edwin, too. Right as he pulled himself to his feet, the door squeaked open again. Marcus held his breath.

"It's me," Edwin called, his voice croaking concerningly, but at least he was alive.

Relief turned Marcus's legs to jam, and he almost collapsed. But he straightened his spine and slipped out from behind the crates. "What happened? What took you so long?"

He swept his gaze over his friend, frowning. Blood stained Edwin's clothes, but he didn't see any wounds, and there was also fresh dirt and mud.

"You're dead," Edwin said. He cleared his throat. "I borrowed a horse to go to the woods beyond the field . . . where I buried you. If anyone digs it up, they'll find a sack of dried beans stolen from the barn, so hopefully no one does. Then I returned to the inn, where thankfully Darius still was—"

"Thankfully?" Marcus's throat went dry. "You idiot! What if he'd killed you?"

"I gambled that he wasn't told to kill me, and it doesn't seem he was. Besides, he was still arguing with the innkeeper to untie him. Seems the innkeeper was so incensed over the damage done to his floors, he'd gagged the assassin and was planning to send for a sheriff. The assassin worked off the gag, but the innkeeper wasn't buying that he was sent by the new king."

Marcus leaned against the stack of crates. "So . . . you told him he'd succeeded?"

"I acted like I wanted to attack Darius, then made a scene of cursing him and mourning you and drinking and talking about burying you in the forest." He smiled, but red rimmed his puffy eyes. "I regret I had to lose more of our things to cover the drink, but I needed to look convincingly distraught. It wasn't difficult, thinking about seeing you unmoving in a puddle of blood."

It took a moment for Marcus to speak. He couldn't imagine how he would have felt in Edwin's place. "That was reckless."

"Why do you think I didn't tell you my plan?"

He shook his head, wincing at the pain that stabbed through his forehead. "Did it at least work?"

"I hope so." Edwin shrugged. "Darius looked smug. There was so much blood on the floor, Marcus . . . it certainly looked like someone could have died. Darius paid for the damage and left. I checked the stables before coming back in, and one of the horses is gone. He seemed convinced, but we'll need to keep you out of sight for a bit, just in case. Now. Let's find some light and get a look at that cut."

Thankfully, the bleeding had mostly stopped. The wound was far smaller than either of them had expected, and Edwin decided to forgo stitches. Instead, he snuck back into the kitchen, where he stole a bowl of water, some honey, a couple of bread rolls, and even found a bit of dried yarrow.

"We have to pay them," Marcus protested. "I don't want to harm my own—"

"It isn't much. Two rolls, a pinch of yarrow, and a spoonful of honey won't ruin them, and I'll return the spoon and bowl. But I can't tell them what I need, or they'll be suspicious, so I had to grab everything while no one was looking. Besides, I overpaid for those bereavement drinks. All right?"

Begrudgingly, Marcus agreed. Edwin cut a strip of cloth off one of his undertunics, despite Marcus's protests. Placing the dried yarrow on the cloth, he used the back of the spoon to grind the herb into a coarse powder. After he cleaned Marcus's face, the cut began bleeding again, but considerably less than before. Edwin smeared the wound with the yarrow to slow the bleeding and then with honey to protect against infection, and finally wrapped Marcus's head again with the cloth strip. This bandage was much neater and smaller, leaving his vision unimpeded.

They ate the rolls and then dozed off and on for the rest of the day, partly burrowed into the hay in the barn. Despite being itchy, it was fairly warm. Whenever anyone entered, they covered themselves with hay. When darkness fell, they brushed the hay off their clothing, tied their blanket packs on under their cloaks, and headed out.

To Marcus's surprise, Edwin had also managed to keep the bread the innkeeper had given them, and they split that while they walked. Although the cut still stung and he had a tender spot on the right side of his head, Marcus was fine—at least physically.

Inside, he felt hollow.

A little past the edge of town, Marcus stopped to look back. He had a gut feeling he wouldn't return. The ruined castle beyond the town was no longer home, and Alimer Principality no longer existed.

With a mixture of sorrow and tired acceptance, he let being an Alimer prince go, and turned his back on the town and the dark plume of smoke that obscured the stars. Ahead of him was Adriana, if she still lived, but the idea brought equal anticipation and anxiety.

What if, after four years, Adriana had reached the same conclusion as the innkeeper? What if she had realized he was a coward who had only publicly confessed his love and admitted to their relationship when he was backed into a corner by an arranged marriage?

His only comfort was that if Darius truly had been fooled, he would report to King Mortimer that he had succeeded in his task, and Mortimer wouldn't be looking for him.

Because assassination attempt or no, Marcus still needed to know if Adriana was alive and well.

CHAPTER 7

Cattle didn't have any right to make Marcus as emotional as they did.

Across the wide, snow-covered field, a herd of cattle grazed on the other side of a log fence. Notches in the cattle's ears marked them as belonging to the Faine family, and the sight roused precious memories of visiting the same herd with Adriana. After two days of travel, they were getting close to Faine Castle.

Marcus and Edwin had opted to take a less direct route toward Faine Castle that was much hillier, longer, and colder than Marcus remembered. Of course, he'd never traveled so far on foot before, either—and never while unarmed. They'd heard wolves in the distance one night when they hadn't made it to the next town before nightfall, but they'd encountered only a few deer and startled rabbits. Once he could have sworn that he saw a unicorn disappearing into the trees, but Edwin insisted unicorns didn't bound like deer.

At least the cold brought the reassurance that the great bears were hibernating. The deadly beasts towered above any man, even Marcus with his above-average height, and that was before adding in the horns. They usually preferred the small mountain range in the north, though, and the great bears that ventured into the forests always retreated to the mountains to hibernate. One less thing that might want to kill him.

To avoid drawing the attention of the humans who wanted Marcus dead, Edwin had bought all of their supplies when they stopped in small towns, and Marcus mostly kept to himself at the inns, avoiding the curious stares his bandaged head attracted. Now that his cut had scabbed over, he no longer needed the bandage, and thankfully, no one appeared to be looking for him.

Reaching the Faine's herd almost made up for the long day of walking through snow flurries and munching on biscuits that had a suspicious similarity to rocks. Marcus had been trudging through the powdery snow, his gloved hands shoved under his armpits for warmth and his head bowed to minimize snowflakes drifting into his face, when he'd heard the low of cattle. It was already midafternoon, and they shouldn't waste daylight, but for a few minutes, he stood rooted in place.

The cattle's long, gently curved horns swayed with their peaceful movement, and their shaggy reddish-brown fur looked unfairly warm and cozy. Three calves pranced through the snow. They were at least a few months old, likely already weaned, but still smaller, and their fur appeared softer than that of the older cattle.

Adriana had often used visiting these cattle as an excuse to leave the castle and secretly meet with Marcus. She still always wanted to actually watch the cattle, especially during calving season. He never minded, because he loved the way her eyes lit up every time she saw them, especially if there were any new calves. Adriana called the cattle "fluffy cows" because that's what her mother had called them, and she declared there was nothing as precious and huggable as a tiny long-haired calf with its fuzzy hair.

They'd spent hours watching the cattle and talking. Sometimes they had shared memories of their mothers. While Marcus's mother had died from a septic wound when he was ten, Adriana's mother had passed from a wasting illness only a few months before they'd met. He'd sympathized with her grief and was the listening ear she needed. They both found it easier to process their sorrow and retell the stories of love and laughter with someone outside of their family—although Adriana's older brother, Jairus, sounded much kinder and easier to talk to than Marcus's brothers had been. They'd shared so many secrets and emotional conversations, all covered by the lowing of cattle.

While stuck in that tower, Marcus had frequently pictured himself right where he now stood, with Adriana at his side. She would laugh as a couple of energetic calves playfully butted heads and then ran off, kicking up their muddy hooves.

He blinked away tears. Perhaps he could blame the wetness on snowflakes melting on his face, but that wasn't it. Missing Adriana was a gaping pit deep inside him that he didn't know how to close.

"We should continue," Edwin commented, breaking the silence. "If we don't slow down, we should be able to reach Glenborough by sundown."

Marcus took a deep breath and nodded. "If there's any news to be had about Adriana, it'll have made its way there."

"And then what?" Edwin asked quietly.

Adjusting his pack and cloak, Marcus started forward again. "We look for work, I suppose."

"So close to Faine Castle?"

"I don't really know yet." The truth was he wasn't ready to think about it yet. Because if he thought about it, he'd have to decide what to do if Adriana no longer wanted to own cattle with him.

As they left the cattle behind, Marcus cast one last look back at them, and hoped whatever news they found in Glenborough would be good.

Finding a table directly in front of the fire at one of Glenborough's two inns seemed the best stroke of luck Marcus had been blessed with in years. He sighed contentedly as he sank into the chair opposite Edwin and sprawled out his limbs, basking in the warmth and the comforting cackle.

The snow had picked up, and a frigid wind had started shortly before sunset. With this spot by the fire, he was comfortably warm and would soon be dry.

Edwin had traded their last silver candlestick for dinner, a night's boarding, and breakfast the next morning. He looked at Marcus glumly as the barmaid thunked down two tankards of ale and hurried away.

"We might be able to trade some of our clothing, but I think after this we'll have to trade our labor or find employment."

Marcus shrugged as he dragged his tankard toward himself. "As we knew we would. We'll figure it out."

A group of three men entered, snow blowing around them before they slammed the door shut. One of them called out to the innkeeper like they were old friends, and the three occupied the table behind Marcus.

"Seems a mighty rush is all I'm saying," one of the men said. "He's not been king for even a month yet. I'd think he'd be more worried about that than weddings."

"No, see, I think that's why," another man said, his tone insistent. "How much men and wealth do you reckon King Mortimer lost suppressing the other two princes?"

"Probably less than he gained by becoming king," snorted the third.

"But think about it. I hear the man's rich—"

"How does that help the king? He should marry off his son for a good dowry if he needs to refill his treasury, not his daughter."

Marcus choked on his ale, spewing some across the table. Edwin leaned back with a disgusted expression. The barmaid approached their table, their supper in hand, and eyed the droplets sprayed across the tabletop with distaste as she set down their servings of steak and ale pie. But he was too focused on the conversation at the table behind him to care about Edwin's or the barmaid's judgment.

"Sure, but do you think it works the same when you're marrying the king's only daughter?" The speaker scoffed. "This lord is probably paying a bride price to the king for the honor of marrying the princess."

Edwin froze with his fork halfway to his mouth, and their eyes met. So he'd heard the same thing. Marcus wished he hadn't. He could have imagined he'd misheard or misunderstood.

"Personally, I don't care what the reason is," one of the speakers declared. "Once she's wed, it's unlikely to affect us common folk. But the wedding itself will mean a feast for all the area surrounding the castle, if His Majesty follows tradition. I don't worry myself with things above my place, like who or why Princess Adriana is marrying. But I'll never say no to free food."

"Hear, hear!" Laughing and the clacking together of tank-ards followed.

Despite the crackling fire, Marcus had gone cold. A single tear raced down his nose and splashed into his ale.

"Marcus . . ."

He shook his head. Whatever condolences or wisdom Edwin might offer, he wasn't in the mood to hear it.

What had he expected? That after four years of separation and after he was reduced to a pauper—and likely presumed dead—Adriana wouldn't move on? That she'd remain single for the rest of her days? He should be wishing her happiness as well as security in her marriage to someone far more suitable than him, but all he could feel was the crushing weight of heartbreak.

CHAPTER 8

There had been days in the tower when Marcus didn't want to rise in the morning. Why should he leave his comfortable bed to face another day of monotony with little to do and nowhere to go but up and down the same spiral staircase? Eventually, his stomach, the call of nature, Edwin knocking on his door, or the thought of Adriana had gotten him out of bed. After all, how could he lie there and waste away when he had promised her that one day, he would marry her?

How he hated the pain in his heart and the swell of unrighteous fury toward this nameless lord that the woman he loved more than life itself was going to marry.

The castle wasn't far. He could go to her, sneak in like he had before, and ask if she really wanted this marriage. She'd promised never to give up on him . . .

"Marcus."

He stared at the candlelight flickering on the wall and ignored Edwin.

"I know you're awake. It's getting late. We paid for breakfast, so we should get it." When Marcus still didn't move, Edwin sighed. "I'm sorry. I know it's not the news you wanted, and you're hurting. But you shouldn't give up."

"On her?" Marcus asked without lifting his head from the thin excuse of a pillow.

"On living." The floorboards creaked softly as Edwin shifted, then he sat on the edge of the bed. "She's marrying a wealthy lord. I think . . . I think you should give up on her. She's clearly given up on you."

Tears threatened again, so he squeezed his eyes shut. After a couple of steadying breaths, he opened his eyes and said, "But what if she would choose me if she knew I'm alive? Or what if it's an arranged marriage she doesn't want, just like I didn't want mine? Shouldn't I fight for her and not . . ." He gulped. "Not be a coward? Again?"

After a moment, Edwin spoke quietly. "It's not cowardice to be wise. Haven't you said before Mortimer seems to truly love his children?"

"Yes." He'd been jealous of Adriana's relationship with her father more than once.

"Do you really think her father would force her into a marriage she doesn't want?"

Marcus gripped his blanket with clenched fists. His own father may have tried to force him into a marriage and imprisoned him when he refused, but Mortimer wasn't Arlius. Adriana must have accepted this marriage, or it wouldn't be happening. At worst, that meant she no longer loved him. At best, it meant she'd made peace with his death, and letting her know he was alive might distress her.

"And what's the alternative?" Edwin asked. "You run away together? You both always talked about peace. If her father did arrange this marriage, it must be for the good of the kingdom. Meanwhile, I'm sorry, Marcus, but the son of Mortimer's vanquished rival stealing away his daughter days before her wedding is unlikely to benefit Aedyllan's peace and prosperity. If he sent an assassin after you before you did anything, he'll send an army after you for disappearing with his daughter. Anyone who doesn't support him might think you're making a bid for the throne, and you'll find yourself in the middle of a war. And you won't even have anywhere to take her."

Marcus sat up and rested his forearms on his knees but avoided looking at Edwin. He certainly didn't want to start another war. His heart screamed that Edwin was wrong, but at the same time, what he said made sense.

To marry Adriana, Marcus had only two options. First, he could run away with her, right at the start of winter with no money and nowhere to live, likely irreparably damaging her relationship with the father she loved, potentially throwing all of Aedyllan into chaos, and spending every day waiting for another assassin to appear. That was assuming she even agreed.

She might choose her betrothed, whoever he was, because that marriage was free of such risks. A wealthy lord could provide for Adriana and protect her in a way Marcus couldn't.

Second, he could reveal himself to King Mortimer and—in the event he wasn't killed the moment he revealed his identity—attempt to convince the king to not only let him live but also grant him Adriana's hand in marriage and a holding so he could be worthy of her and provide for her. Why would Mortimer do that when Adriana had already agreed to a far more advantageous marriage?

Either course of action had an uncomfortably high chance of ending with Marcus's death.

"So it's better for her if I leave her alone?" That didn't feel right at all, and yet . . . it would be safer and easier. He wouldn't have to risk hearing Adriana tell him she didn't love him anymore. If he didn't try, he couldn't be executed for his failure.

Best to stay out of Adriana's way. As his father had said, that was all he was good at.

"Let her be happy," Edwin said. "And make the choice that keeps you alive."

Marcus nodded. It shattered his heart, but he cut the last thread that connected him to who he had been as Prince Marcus Alimer.

No family.

No home.

No crown.

And no lover waiting for his return.

"Will you come eat now?" Edwin prodded. "You didn't finish your supper, so you must be hungry."

Marcus didn't want to eat, but if he said that, Edwin would argue that his body needed food, even if he was too dejected to pay attention. He sighed. "If I must."

His friend stood. "You must."

Marcus groaned and threw his legs over the side of the bed, but his shoulders slumped as he searched for the motivation to move farther than that. "Sorry. I must seem pathetic."

"Yes." Edwin smirked when Marcus looked up in shock. "Your hair's a tangled mess. Half the braids are falling out. Absolutely pathetic appearance." His expression softened. "But it's not pathetic to have a broken heart. I'd be more worried about you if you didn't care."

Before they went down to breakfast, Edwin insisted on doing Marcus's braids "so they aren't lopsided again." As that was a fair criticism, Marcus let him. After changing into their cleanest outfits, they went to the dining room on the ground floor. There were many empty tables despite how busy the inn had been the night before and how many of the beds had been occupied in the large, shared room where they'd slept. They turned in their breakfast tokens and placed their order—the barkeep muttered something under his breath about late-comers—and settled in at a table near the fireplace.

"How does one look for work?" Marcus thrummed his fingers on the tabletop.

"Are you sure you're ready for that?"

"It's better than sitting here weeping all day, right?" Truthfully, if he didn't find a new path for his life soon, he might lose the will to do so.

"Inns and taverns are places where news is exchanged." Edwin shrugged. "Maybe the barkeep will know of anyone who is hiring."

Unfortunately, the barkeep didn't have any leads. Worse, he warned that they might have difficulty finding an open position, especially a high-paying one. Many servants and workers had been released in the aftermath of the fighting, as the conflict had caused a slow in farming production, the onset of winter was rarely a time anyone was looking to hire, and many lesser noble households had lost men and thus had to reduce their staff.

So Marcus and Edwin moved to the market, where they spent two cold hours being told no one was hiring or only one-time tasks were available. Stops at two small taverns turned up only employment that afforded no housing. As they tromped across Glenborough through dirty slush to the other, more expensive inn, Marcus was preparing to resign himself to a difficult winter of living meal-to-meal and hoping they could afford to live at an inn.

Another reason to be grateful Adriana was marrying someone capable of providing for her, even if it still hurt like frostbite.

The harried-looking innkeeper at the White Swan inn and tavern gave them an appraising look when they inquired if he knew of anyone hiring, especially hiring servants. He directed them to a finely dressed man sitting in the back corner of the tavern, his forehead scrunched as he made notes in a ledger.

"Pardon me." Marcus bowed.

The man looked up and blinked at them for several moments. He shook his head, his brown hair catching on the velvet of his overtunic. "Yes?"

"We were told you're hiring household servants?"

"Ah, good; yes!" The man looked them up and down with a critical eye, and Marcus was glad he'd let Edwin do his hair and had put on a tunic that wasn't completely mud-splattered. "I'm Steward Talwen, manager of Lord Lucien Thorne's household."

The name wasn't familiar, but he'd never kept up with all of the nobility, especially not outside of Alimer Principality.

"My esteemed lord is looking for servants to do various tasks as required of them." Talwen stood and walked around them, then, to Marcus's bemusement, squeezed their upper arms. "Smile." Uncertainly, Marcus complied, and Talwen glanced between him and Edwin, then gave a satisfied nod. "My lord should find you acceptable. You both look the part of a noble's servants, and don't appear to be weaklings, pipe addicts, sluggards, or drunkards. Do you have experience in a noble household?"

"Yes," Marcus and Edwin said together. This could be perfect—Edwin was well acquainted with serving a nobleman, and while Marcus would find the serving part new, he was familiar with the expectations of the noble lifestyle.

"Why did you leave your previous employment?"

"Death in the noble family," Marcus said. "As a result of the war."

"Ah." Steward Talwen nodded. "You're available to start immediately, then? And amiable to moving far?"

"Yes." Relief crashed through Marcus. The further away from Glenborough and Faine Castle, the better.

"We depart Glenborough this afternoon. Is that acceptable?"

"Yes," Marcus said. That was even better.

"Excellent." Talwen flipped through his ledger to a collection of loose papers covered in writing and pulled out two. "Employment contract. My lord values loyalty, so he requires an agreement to serve for five years. You'll be paid ten silver coins monthly, be given room and board, and be provided with clothing. Lord Thorne won't be humiliated by shabby servants.

If you wish to terminate your contract before the five years are completed, you must pay a contract severance debt of one hundred gold. Should my lord find your service untenable and release you early, he will pay you an extra month's wages."

Marcus nearly choked, and he heard Edwin make a sound of surprise as well. At three silver coins to one gold coin, one hundred gold would be . . . two and a half years' worth of wages. Half of the entire contract amount.

"That . . . doesn't seem fair," Edwin said.

"Do you plan on abandoning your new employment so soon? Then perhaps we do not want you, anyway."

"Could you give us a moment?" Marcus caught Edwin's eye and nodded away from the table.

The steward huffed. "Very well."

They withdrew a couple of paces, and Marcus spoke in a whisper. "Do you think it's a bad idea?" He hoped his disappointment wasn't too obvious. If Edwin saw a problem, he should listen. Still, these positions would solve so many of their troubles . . .

Edwin rubbed his chin. "Your father paid me only eight silver pieces a month in addition to housing, food, and my garments, so it's generous in that regard. However, I've never heard of a contract with such a high breaking fee. I initially had a four-year contract with a severance debt if I broke it early, but it was six months' wages, so it was more possible to leave.

Aside from the fact that this contract ends in five years, it practically sounds like a clever way of circumventing Aedyllan's laws prohibiting slavery."

"Ah." Despite himself, Marcus's shoulders slumped. "Then is it better to continue to search?" And hope they didn't freeze to death, but he kept that to himself.

Edwin sighed, his expression glum. "Five years of nearly guaranteed food, shelter, and income sounds better than our current predicament, and I'm happy to get you far from Faine Castle. But we'll be trapped if this lord turns out to be a monster. Although, I doubt a monster would pay extra wages when he dismisses a servant. Your father withheld any owed payments when a servant was dismissed. It may be a risk worth taking."

Turning this over in his mind, Marcus nodded back toward the steward.

"Well?" Steward Talwen asked at their approach.

"A question, if you don't mind."

"Of course."

"You asked why we left our last employment. Why did your lord's previous servants leave?"

By the wide-eyed stare Talwen gave him, that was not considered an appropriate question.

"If you must know"—his tone dripped condescension—"this opportunity is available to you because my lord recently improved his status and thus requires a larger and more digni-fied household than he'd previously kept. You aren't replace-ments, but new additions."

Strange. How did a lord suddenly find his status so im-proved he needed to expand the size of his household? Perhaps for the same reason other households had released servants—war. This lord must have aided King Mortimer, which would also explain why he was passing through Glenborough on his way back home.

He looked to Edwin, who nodded once as an unspoken understanding passed between them. It wasn't ideal, but they'd take it. Anything for some certainty . . . and to leave Glenbor-ough before Adriana's wedding.

CHAPTER 9

"Marcus and Edwin Williams." Lord Thorne surveyed them with the expression of someone evaluating livestock.

Marcus tried not to look like he was assessing right back. Lord Lucien Thorne was likely in his mid to late twenties. The top half of his shoulder-blade-length brown hair was plaited along the sides of his head in several multistrand braids, a declaration of status—no man who worked for a living had the time to put that much effort into his hair. His bright-blue overtunic was spotless even down to the hem that brushed his boots, and wolf fur trimmed the thick cloak thrown over his seatback. As he shifted his attention to Edwin, candlelight gleamed on the curling end of an unornamented silver hair stick that was stuck through the leather lacing that tied his braids together at the crown of his head.

If all of that wasn't enough to shout his wealth, they were currently in the largest single-bed lodging in the White Swan. The room boasted its own table and chairs and a wardrobe. It had to cost a hefty sum—to say nothing of paying for wherever the rest of Thorne's attendants were staying.

"Yes, you'll do. Much better chosen this time, Talwen." Thorne gave a satisfied nod. "I was beginning to worry. I couldn't possibly arrive with insufficient staff. Usually I like a few reliable servants, but with my new status, that simply won't do. I have expectations to meet—which means you do as well." He sniffed and waved at their clothing. "This disheveled mess is unacceptable. Steward, find these men some less travel-worn clothing."

Steward Talwen bowed, and Marcus and Edwin followed his lead before trailing him out of Lord Thorne's chamber.

"We'll get several garments ordered and tailored to you both after we arrive at Thorne's castle, but in the meantime, we have some extra clothing that should suffice until you get your own things washed." Talwen led them to a large room with ten cots, on a few of which lounged men of varying ages in the fine but simple clothing of servants. "These are some of your fellow servants."

Talwen waved in the general direction of some of the other men. They returned Marcus's polite nod. The steward directed them to several trunks in the back of the room. They found long-sleeved undershirts and tunics that weren't much too small and that satisfied Talwen.

"Good. Add those to your belongings and try to keep them looking fresh so you can change into them when we arrive. If you have any other belongings, get them here quickly. We'll be packing up within the hour."

A couple of hours later, they were trekking through muddy slush along the road. Four knights rode horses, while their new liege rode comfortably inside a carriage. Steward Talwen must have been inside as well, because Marcus didn't see him. But Marcus, Edwin, and the other servants—five men and four women—were stuck soaking their boots and tiring their legs.

Marcus drifted closer to another servant, a middle-aged man whose long blond hair was neatly pinned back with a wooden clasp. "Hello. I'm Marcus."

The man inclined his head. "Roger. Nice to meet you."

"So . . . perhaps an embarrassing question, but where exactly does Lord Thorne live?"

Roger raised an eyebrow. "Desperate for work, eh?" He shrugged. "I understand; I've been there before. Lord Thorne's castle is on the western side of what used to be Nydellan Principality. Haven't heard what it's called now."

Marcus frowned. That didn't make sense for the road they were traveling, which passed Faine Castle on the route north. He'd been disappointed when he realized which road they were taking, but maybe this meant they'd turn before they reached the castle. "Then where are we going now?"

"Where . . ." Roger laughed. "Oh, son. Are you in for a

surprise. We'll be staying in the king's castle for a few days, until after the wedding. Then Lord Thorne will take us and his new bride back home. Steward Talwen is on his way to Lord Thorne's estate to prepare it for the newlyweds' arrival."

A sinking feeling settled into the pit of Marcus's stomach, and when he spoke, his voice cracked. "Bride?"

"Aye. Lord Thorne is marrying Princess Adriana Faine."

Dazed, Marcus drifted over to Edwin, whose face had gone white as the snow blanketing the surrounding hills.

"What do we do?" Edwin whispered.

He shook his head, too in shock to begin to formulate his fragmented thoughts into coherent speech.

What *could* they do? They didn't have any gold to give Lucien Thorne to break their contract and no idea what would happen if they tried to run away. Likely the mounted knights would drag them back, and Lord Thorne could punish them however he liked—and they didn't know the man well enough to know what that might look like. Perhaps they could even be imprisoned for reneging on the contract while unable to pay the debt. Could a man be hanged for such a large debt? It wasn't a concern Marcus had ever had before.

At least King Mortimer was highly unlikely to recognize him, but Adriana would. Her handmaiden, Leena, almost certainly would as well. What if one of them said something? And what about Darius? If the assassin lived in Faine Castle and spotted him, Marcus's life would be over. Perhaps running was the safer option, even if it came with uncertainties.

Still . . .

If he stayed, he would get to see Adriana. He could watch her interact with her bridegroom and maybe, if he saw her happy, it would ease some of the pain in his own heart.

But he couldn't stay and watch her be married to another man for the next five years.

Gradually and hopefully imperceptibly, they drifted toward the rear and side of the small procession, hopefully out of earshot, but Marcus still whispered. "Do you think they'd notice if we ran?"

"Probably," Edwin murmured. "Maybe not right away, but soon enough those knights could easily run us down. I fear we have no choice but to wait to escape from the castle and hope we can get enough of a head start they won't catch us quickly. Surely they'd abandon the chase so as not to distract from the wedding, and we can be long gone. Maybe even go to Eynlae or Talland."

Wedding was like a punch to Marcus's gut, but somehow, he kept walking. "For today, we'll simply have to stay in the background and avoid Adriana and Leena as much as possible."

"And hope to the ends of Miraveld that Darius isn't in Faine Castle," Edwin muttered.

Marcus stared at the sludge-filled ruts and bits of murky

ice in the road. Some part of his mind suggested he give up and collapse. His emotions were too tumultuous, his desires too scattered, and all the bad news from the last week piled onto him, pressing him toward the dirt. A numbness spread through his body, and although he kept putting one foot in front of the other, it was without conscious thought, as if something else was making his limbs move.

Something bumping against his shoulder and Edwin's voice startled him back to the present.

"Are you going to be all right?" Edwin whispered.

Marcus blinked, taking in the castle that had appeared in front of them, towering over the landscape. The path ahead wove past trees and bushes up a tall hill to the base of Faine Castle, an imposing square with round towers for stairs at all four corners and in the middle of the front and the back. Shale tiles covered the conical roofs of the towers and the two long gables forming the castle's roof. Pairs of massive chimneys sprouted from the right and left ends of the roof, and another chimney rose between the gables in the center. Thin arrowslits marked the towers, and the wood shutters covering the windows in the walls of the castle were all shut fast—except . . .

Marcus blinked. The road curved enough he got a glimpse of the left side of the castle, where a snowy trellis with dormant vines stretched up over the stones to a window on the third floor . . . that was open. A bit of orangish light in the dark opening made him certain of it. Adriana had once promised she would never latch those shutters or cover the window for the winter in case he ever visited her. His heart twisted painfully, and he nearly tripped over the uneven surface of the road.

What did it mean, that as her betrothed arrived, even after her father had sent an assassin to kill him, Adriana had not sealed her window despite the cold? He didn't know, and he hated the irrational thrill of hope that went through him. She deserved a husband as securely wealthy as Thorne, and Aedyllan needed stability more than Marcus needed Adriana. Shaking away futile dreams, he focused on navigating the muddy road.

There was no longer an icicle's chance in a dragon's cave for Marcus to have a future with Adriana.

Yet as they approached the castle, his heart beat faster. Every step took him nearer to the snow-dusted stone staircase. Soon he was standing in front of the stairs' flared base and elegant stone balustrade that curved around a short decorative column. He looked up the steps that ran up the wall to an arched doorway in the central tower.

He was going to see Adriana for the first time in far too many years.

Edwin leaned close and whispered, "Whatever happens, I'll stand by you."

Marcus mumbled his thanks. He didn't plan on getting

caught—or falling to pieces when he saw Adriana—but it was reassuring to know his friend would have his back and understood his inner turmoil.

Servants led away the horses and carriage to the stables at the rear of the castle. Thorne's servants grouped together behind the knights, who took up position following their lord. Marcus kept his hood up and slouched to make his tall frame smaller as they entered Faine Castle.

CHAPTER 10

Marcus had climbed the trellis.

Leafy vines slick from the afternoon's summer rain covered the trellis that sprawled up the side of the castle to her window on the third floor. But he'd climbed it, just as he'd promised he would in his last letter.

Adriana stared at him in the flickering light of the candle on the table, moonlight limning his frame and highlighting his dark hair. Was he taller than she remembered? He made her feel so tiny.

It had been over a month since they'd last met up, as it was difficult for Marcus to explain disappearing by himself for a day at a time to his father. Some days Adriana despised Prince Arlius for keeping them apart.

"You came," she whispered.

Marcus grinned, a softness in his eyes that sent her heart racing. "You asked me to."

A blush crept over her cheeks. "I didn't?"

"'I wish I could see you,'" he quoted her letter. "So far as it is in my power, I'll grant your every wish."

Adriana's knees went weak. A sudden need filled her, the tipping point of months of longing. She reached out and grabbed the front of his long tunic and pulled him close. He must have wanted the same thing she did, because then his lips were on hers, his fingers tangled in her tresses and hers gripping his silky hair.

Her first kiss wasn't as magical as she'd thought it'd be—it was fumbling and awkward. There were a few ows when their teeth knocked together, or his hand got stuck in her curls, but they soon found a rhythm. When they separated, both breathing a little harder, she rested her palms on his chest and looked up into his brown eyes.

Her mind warned perhaps this was too big of a promise for two almost-seventeen-year-olds who weren't even supposed to see each other, but her heart knew what it wanted.

"I wish to kiss only you for the rest of my days, Marcus Alimer."

A knock sounded on Adriana's chamber door. She considered saying she was indecent and whoever it was couldn't enter, but if it was Father, that'd only make his impending lecture worse. Before she had a chance to respond, the door opened, prompting a frown from her maidservant, Leena, that the young woman quickly hid.

"Adri—" A heavy sigh marked Jairus's entrance.

She turned away from her open window and the snow-covered landscape beyond it and faced her older brother.

"You can't wear that. And how many times have you been told to cover that window for the season? You're going to catch cold."

"My plant needs the sunshine." She motioned toward the gooseberry plant in its pot atop a small stand next to her door. It had been a gift from Leena's grandfather, Alban, the castle healer, after six-year-old Adriana had been jealous of his room full of medicinal plants and begged for one for her room. "Besides, I like the view."

Very few of the rooms in the castle had a window, as most of the windows instead opened to the enclosed halls that ran around the perimeter. Adriana was lucky enough to have a room on the end of the third floor, and she cherished that window far too much to cover it with a tapestry for the winter. Both the view and the memories it held were too precious, and she'd made a promise . . . even if promises mattered little when only one person was alive to care.

She moved to sit on the edge of her bed, its heavy curtains currently tied back to the posts. "As for my gown, I'm in mourning. Why shouldn't I wear black?"

Jairus hung his head but quickly straightened with a frown. He pushed his gold circlet back into its proper place across his forehead, then his fingertips brushed where the ends of the circlet tucked into his multistrand braids. She reflected distantly that her brother cared more about how she looked when meeting her betrothed than she did.

"Ri . . ." Jairus sat on the bed next to her. "It's bad luck to—"

"I don't care." There was no force behind the words. Only the numbness that had settled into her after days of weeping.

He fell silent for a moment. "I don't say this to be harsh or disregard your sorrow and loss, sister. Marcus is gone, and you're going to spend the rest of your life with Lucien. Is this truly how you want your relationship to start? With disrespect by wearing an unlucky color of mourning to your first meeting? Will you tell him why and bring your past love into your marriage like a specter? Or do you perhaps think this will cause him to retract his offer of marriage? Because it won't, Ri. You stand a higher chance of ending up with a husband who dislikes you than of having no husband."

"And how can you stand by and be all right with that?"

Adriana shoved to her feet, her back to her brother to hide the tears welling along her eyelids. Maybe she wasn't completely numb. "How can—"

"I've tried to talk to Father," Jairus said quietly. "I'm not all right with it, but there's nothing I can do. I've even tried to convince him to arrange a marriage for me instead, but he says there's no reason to take the time to search for a fitting, wealthy young lady and come to an agreement when he has a wealthy and willing lord at the ready. He's forbidden me to broach the subject again."

"Thank you for trying," she whispered. She wrapped her arms around her middle, resignation a yawning chasm in her very soul.

Soft footsteps whispered across the rug, then a hand rested on her shoulder. "Lord Thorne's entourage has been spotted. He'll arrive soon. Please change quickly and come down to the hall to greet your bridegroom."

"You came so Father wouldn't, didn't you?"

In response, her brother only squeezed her shoulder.

Once, Father had been kind, doting even. Strict when necessary, but always loving. While she didn't truly doubt her father's love now, he had changed over the war—and since he'd received some secret prophecy from that fae woman. The fighting and utter annihilation of the other princes' families had hardened him, leaving a darkness in his eyes and a shadow over his heart. The fae's blessing had made him cocky. At the same time, the knowledge such powerful magic might have a steep price in the distant future also made him paranoid.

He ruled Aedyllan unchallenged, but at a cost to his coffers, his military, and his soul. Lord Lucien Thorne, Father had told her, had been a valiant and unstoppable force on the battlefield, and he had something the royal treasury needed—money.

Kings had to make cold calculations, he said. If that meant murdering the man his daughter loved because he was the sole remaining heir of his rivals, so be it. If it meant marrying off his only daughter against her wishes because the groom had offered a large bride-price, so be it. A woman's heart had no role to play in the games of kings.

"Please, Ri," Jairus whispered. "Don't make this harder on yourself."

Her shoulders slumped, and she nodded. "All right."

He pressed a quick kiss to her temple, and his long, wavy blond hair brushed against her cheek. "I'll see you downstairs shortly."

After changing into a more appropriate, bright-green gown, Adriana wrapped herself in a white cloak lined with white rabbit fur and donned a silver circlet, then headed downstairs. Father looked up as she entered the great hall, the crease between his eyebrows beneath his gold crown easing.

"Adriana, good." Father waved her over to stand at his left side on the dais, where he stood in front of his throne.

She didn't acknowledge him as she took her place, still unable to speak to him after what he'd done.

Jairus sent her an encouraging smile, but she didn't have the strength to smile back. She buried her heart, locking up her emotions deep down so she wouldn't break when she met the man she was to marry, and he wasn't Marcus.

Knights and servants lined the walls of the great hall. Every candle in the wall sconces, two massive iron chandeliers, and the candlesticks on the two long rows of tables were lit. Fires blazed in the gigantic fireplace at the far end of the hall next to the main entrance and in the smaller fireplace to the side of the dais. She didn't need her cloak with all that heat, but the stairwells and halls held a chill. The ostentation almost made her roll her eyes. What was the point of putting on this show when the entire reason for this marriage was that the king needed to refill his treasury?

At last, the great door swung open. The herald entered and announced Lord Lucien Thorne, then withdrew to join the other watching servants.

A man strode in, snow melting on his clothing. An assortment of retainers followed him in and respectfully shuffled off to the side as the door was drawn closed behind them. Adriana focused on the man, her betrothed.

He was tall, perhaps only slightly taller than average, but with a ground-eating stride and a muscular build that made him feel larger. The top of his brown hair was done in an intricate multitude of braids that put Father's and Jairus's to shame. For a warrior who had distinguished himself on the battlefield, he had a surprisingly pale face—shaven, smooth, and unblemished. The sword at his side stuck out from beneath his black, fur-trimmed cloak, and intricate embroidery decorated the bright-blue overtunic that fell to his ankles.

Lucien stopped a pace or so before the dais and swept into a bow, flourishing his cloak. A silver hair stick with a curved end glinted at the back of his head where his braids were tied together. "Greetings, Your Majesty. Your Highnesses."

"Welcome, Lord Thorne," Father intoned.

Lucien straightened, his piercing blue eyes finding Adriana's rather than her father's as he said, "Thank you, Your Majesty. I'm honored to be welcomed into your home and your family." He gave another, smaller bow. "Greetings, princess."

Somehow, she found her voice. "Welcome, my lord. I'm pleased to finally meet my betrothed." Did she sound as brittle and empty to everyone else as she did to herself? She forced a smile, hoping that would help. She couldn't withstand one of Father's lectures today. "I hope you will rest well tonight, as I look forward to speaking with you tomorrow."

While this was their official introduction, Father had

scheduled her to spend most of the next day with her be-trothed. She was *not* looking forward to it.

At least Lucien was only around six years older than her and handsome enough. He appeared polite. But the thought of marrying him still made her want to retch. She shoved that feeling down as she held her fragile smile in place.

"Thank you, my lady." Lucien smiled, and she likely im-agined it due to her negative mood, but there was something unsettling about that smile. Something predatory and almost mocking. "I look forward to getting to know you as well."

At a wave from Father, several servants escorted Lucien and his knights and servants to their respective quarters. Adriana stared across the hall, ignoring how some of Lucien's servants glanced her way, and worked to keep her calm façade in place until the Faine servants had also filed out of the hall.

She turned to Father and curtsied, preparing to depart.

"You did well," Father said, "if a touch cold. Try to be warmer with him tomorrow." Without waiting for a reply, he swept away, off to deal with whatever matters of putting his newly conquered kingdom together needed his attention now.

Jairus gave her a quick embrace. "Try to give Lucien a chance."

She didn't exactly have a choice, but she nodded.

Up in her room, she cocooned herself in warm blankets and settled onto the cushioned bench in the recess under the open window. Leena brought her supper, which Adriana ate still in front of the window. Sometime later, a gentle shaking awoke her.

"Your Highness." Leena sighed.

Adriana blinked at the darkness. She'd fallen asleep with her head on her arms on the windowsill. She sat up, and Leena brushed her hand over Adriana's curls, flicking away snow.

"It's time for bed," Leena murmured.

Part of Adriana stubbornly didn't want to go to bed, as if somehow, if she didn't go to sleep, tomorrow wouldn't come, and she wouldn't have to face Lucien Thorne and her impending marriage. But she let Leena help her change into a linen night shift. As she crawled into bed, Leena closed the sturdy wood shutters.

"Don't bolt them," Adriana mumbled.

Leena turned away from the window with a sad smile. "I never do, Your Highness."

CHAPTER 11

The castle entrance led straight into a set of narrow, spiraling stairs, but quickly reached a landing. Marcus and Edwin followed the others into a long corridor that cut across the middle of the castle, then through a massive oak door into the great hall. They shuffled off to the side, in the direction of the blessedly warm fire, along with the rest of Thorne's entourage. Lord Thorne strode across the hall to the dais. Peering between the heads of Thorne's servants from where he lurked in the back, Marcus spied Adriana, standing near her father and brother. His breath lodged in his chest. She was even more beautiful than he remembered.

Her thick blonde curls fluffed around her shoulders, and every memory of touching those curls slammed into him at once. A silver circlet glinted on her forehead, but no precious metal could hold a candle to her beautiful face. Her cheeks held a slightly ruddy glow, and her pink lips brought heat to Marcus's skin. A white cloak hung down her back, revealing a bright-green dress that hugged her figure and had elegant long sleeves that cascaded down from her wrists. She looked every inch the princess . . . but she didn't look happy.

Even as Adriana greeted her betrothed, her smile didn't touch her eyes, and her voice lacked its usual liveliness. Perhaps he was seeing what he wished to see, imagining his own feelings in her, but he didn't think so.

Then she said she was pleased to finally meet Lord Thorne. Marcus's hands tightened on the hem of his cloak. How could they be betrothed to be married in only a few days' time if they'd never even met? That man at the tavern had to have been right, and King Mortimer had arranged the marriage because he needed money. *Had* Adriana's father actually forced her to accept this betrothal?

He'd thought it might help if he saw Adriana happy with her betrothed before he disappeared for good.

But if she wasn't happy? If she hadn't accepted this marriage at all, hadn't even been given a choice? The possibility made Marcus's blood boil.

As one of the Faine Castle servants led them from the great hall, Marcus risked glancing at Adriana. She was still smiling, but stared at nothing, the corner of her mouth twitching as if she was struggling to keep the smile in place. He ached for her pain. He'd been in the position of being told he would marry someone he'd never met while his heart belonged to someone else, but he'd known the woman he loved was alive. His refusal had ended in disaster, but he still couldn't believe Mortimer Faine would ignore his daughter's wishes. He lowered his gaze to the floor before he did something stupid like send an outraged glare at the king.

As they were shown to their chambers, were given a tour of the castle, and ate dinner in the cramped servants' dining hall, Marcus turned over this development in his mind. If Adriana wasn't going into this marriage willingly, how could he abandon her? Although he still didn't see another option. Asking her to run away with him to a life as a peasant with no money, shelter from the winter, or even a plan, and with the consequences of breaking his contract with her former betrothed a constant threat, would be foolhardy. But he couldn't do nothing.

He'd done nothing before, and the result had been wasted years, war, death, and now that hollow look in Adriana's false smile.

Marcus only hoped Edwin would understand when he said they couldn't escape yet.

———

"You're a madman," Edwin bit out under his breath.

"Do you have a better idea?" Marcus snapped back.

They sat huddled on a bed in the far corner of the large sleeping quarters they shared with Lord Thorne's male servants. The other servants were talking about the castle, but

Marcus was plotting. Edwin had already guessed that Marcus couldn't abandon Adriana when she didn't look overjoyed to be getting married, and he hadn't objected to staying a while longer. Where he *had* objected was when Marcus proposed breaking into Adriana's room.

"It'll be better if our first meeting is on my terms," Marcus whispered. "It's unlikely we'll be able to avoid both Leena and Adriana, and I don't want Adriana learning the truth from her handmaiden or because she spotted me across the room. Besides, I need to talk to her. I need to confirm she wants to marry Thorne."

"And if the guards catch you?" Edwin asked tightly, eyes flicking to the side to ensure they were still being ignored. "I don't mean to be callous, but she isn't the first person to find themselves in an arranged marriage they don't want. Her father is the king. Thorne would be insane to mistreat her. We, on the other hand, have a very good chance of dying if you're caught."

Marcus stifled his frustration. "One person can sneak into her chamber easier than the two of us can disappear entirely. Besides, we need food at minimum if we're going to get out of here, so we can't leave tonight."

"That's true." Edwin tilted his head. "Do you think she'd pay our debts for breaking the contracts?"

"Maybe." Although Marcus didn't want to ask the woman he loved to help him escape and leave her behind. And if she was marrying Lord Thorne because King Mortimer's treasury was running low, she wouldn't be able to help them with their debts. However, if this convinced Edwin to stop arguing with his plan to approach Adriana, fine. "But to even broach that subject, I have to talk with her in private."

Begrudgingly, Edwin nodded. His gaze searched Marcus's face. "And if she doesn't want Thorne? Are you truly planning on merely talking before we escape?"

"I'm not delusional." Marcus turned away. But he'd be lying if he said he didn't desperately want to know if she still loved him and if she did, he couldn't abandon her—so he didn't say it.

It took forever for the other servants to turn in for the night, and even longer for it to sound like everyone's breathing had deepened to that of sleep—or snores, in a couple of cases. Everyone other than Marcus and Edwin, of course.

Marcus crept past the cots and the slumbering forms of his fellow servants. The room had no windows, but a small fire burned in the fireplace at the opposite end of the room, providing a feeble orange illumination. Edwin propped himself up on one elbow, his expression grim as Marcus opened the door. The hinges creaked softly, but no one stirred. He poked his head out, confirming the hallway was dark and empty, then slipped into the corridor.

This hall ran the length of the rear of the castle. Even though thick, woven tapestries covered all the shuttered windows, the temperature immediately dropped. He shivered and wished he could have brought his cloak, but it would get in the way where he was headed.

Hurrying down the hall, he kept one hand on the outer wall and the other extended in front so he wouldn't run into any walls in the impenetrable blackness. He tiptoed, trying to prevent his boots from clacking against the stone floor. At last, he touched the door at the far end of the hall that opened into the tower with its curving granite staircase. He froze as the door squeaked quietly, but no one shouted or came running, and only the snow-brightened moonlight streaming through the arrowslits provided illumination to the stairwell. No torches or candles announced guards or passing servants.

Rather than climbing the stairs, though, Marcus turned and exited through the door set into the left side of the tower, which opened into another hall. Feeling along the wall, he fumbled for the tapestry covering the first window. It was tricky in the dark, but he freed the bottom two corners from the metal hooks that anchored the hanging and pushed the heavy fabric up. Hints of moonlight showed around the wood shutters. The bolt locking the boards shut was stiff with the cold, but soon he'd swung open the shutters and crawled through the window.

The trellis rose to his right, and he grinned, as happy to see it as he would have been to see an old friend. He shimmied off the sill and grabbed the trellis, avoiding stepping onto the snow. He did not want to leave any footprints. Thankful for the clear night and the bright moonlight reflecting off the snow, he climbed up. While he'd scaled this wall several times, he'd never done so when it was dusted with snow and ice. His gloves quickly soaked through, and his nose was freezing. By the time he reached the window on the third floor, he'd started to shiver.

"Please have kept your promise," Marcus breathed as he stretched toward the shutters. It took his icy fingers a moment to catch the edge of a shutter, but once he did, he tugged and . . .

It swung open. Unlocked.

His heart gave a little leap.

Releasing his pent-up breath, Marcus pushed open the other shutter and carefully hauled himself onto the deep windowsill. This was always his least favorite part, with the greatest chance of something going wrong and sending him tumbling to his death. But he did what he always did during that terrifying moment when he released the trellis and scrambled onto the sill—focused on his love for Adriana instead of his fear of falling.

Within moments, he softly dropped through the opening onto the cushioned bench wedged into the alcove in the wall.

He stepped onto the wood-paneled floor of Adriana's bedroom and stilled. A fire popped quietly in her fireplace across from the window, and the brocade curtains surrounding her bed were drawn closed. She still had that potted plant she loved on a stand next to her door, and for some reason, that made him smile.

What was the best way to go about this? He didn't want to frighten her any more than could be helped. The moonlight from one side and the glowing hearth on the other meant that from either direction, he'd be backlit, merely a looming, dark form pushing aside her curtains. His gaze fell on her little round nightstand, which held a wood cup of water, a clothbound book, a candle on a silver candlestick, and a set of flint. Perfect.

After lighting the candle, he pulled aside the lower half of the two curtains that were drawn along the long side of her bed facing the window—that way, if she was awake, he wouldn't be directly over her. She didn't stir, so he drew back the top curtain and used the cord looped around the post at the head of the bed to tie it open.

Moonlight and candlelight fell across her pillow, creating highlights in her short blonde braid, which her curls were do-ing their best to escape. His throat caught, the ache of forbid-den love settling back in his chest.

Enough standing there and gawking. He wasn't some stalker. Unfortunately, he also needed to make sure she didn't scream and attract the attention of any guards.

Cringing, he eased one knee onto her bed, leaned forward, and pressed his palm over her lips. "Adriana."

She shifted, but the pressure of his hand on her mouth kept her from moving, and her eyes flew open, wide and panicked as she drew in a deep breath through her nose.

"Don't scream—"

Adriana thrashed on the bed and shoved against him, shrieking into his hand.

If she alerted the guards, he'd be dead. He pushed his other hand against her shoulder, trying to force her to still.

"Adriana," he begged, daring to raise his voice above the muffled sound of her attempted scream. "My—" He bit his tongue. It'd been nearly four years, and she was engaged to another. Even if she had left the window unbolted, he had no right to call her beloved. "It's Marcus!"

She stilled, her cry breaking off on a squeak. Her gaze darted over him, and he edged back so they weren't so close and more candlelight fell on his face, but he didn't yet uncover her mouth. Her hands trembled as she gently grabbed his fingers. Holding his breath, he let her pull his hand away.

"Marcus?" Adriana's voice came out strangled and broken.

"Yes." That was all he could get out, his own voice betraying him.

As she sat up, he eased off the edge of the bed, ignoring the twinge of heartbreak when she released him. She seized the candlestick, holding it up between them.

While she studied him, he drank in the sight of her. Although he regretted the shock etched into her pale countenance, she was beautiful. The candle's flame reflected in her hazel eyes, and she was as lovely as she was in his dreams, from her slender fingers on the candlestick to the curls that had escaped her braid, frizzing around her neck, to the definition of her collarbones above her nightgown . . . he forced his gaze back up to her face.

Adriana brushed her fingertips across her lips in a way that had his mind careening toward thoughts of holding and kissing her. But he stood firm where he was.

"Marcus?" A glittering tear squeezed from her eye to trail down the side of her nose. "You—you're—are you . . ." She curled over her stomach with a sob, and Marcus darted forward to take the candle before it could slip from her grasp.

He set it on the nightstand and sat beside her. How he longed to pull her into his arms.

"I thought you died! My father—" She turned away and bit her knuckle, taking in several rasping breaths.

Marcus reached for her but let his hand fall, lost on how to comfort her when he was the reason for her distress.

"I overheard that awful knight telling Father that he . . . he . . ." Tears slid down her cheeks. "He said your companion mourned you; that he saw your grave. But you're alive. You're really real, right?" She tentatively reached toward him, as if afraid he'd turn to smoke.

He took her hand, threading his fingers between hers. "Yes. I'm real, and I'm alive, and I'm here." He gulped. "Is that knight . . . also here?"

"No." She tightened her grip as the word ripped from her in a growl. "I told Father he could force his only daughter to marry some man I don't love, but will he really force me to see the man who murdered my beloved in my own home? He promised that so long as I remain in Faine Castle, that knight won't set a foot within its walls. He sent him to serve another lord for now. Still, I haven't spoken to Father since."

My beloved. She didn't desire this marriage, and she still loved him. But would she feel the same once she understood his current position?

Adriana scooted closer, scrutinizing his forehead. Gingerly, she reached forward and brushed her fingertip over the tiny, faint scar near his temple. "He said he put a dagger through your skull."

Marcus snorted. "He grazed me. It bled enough, though, that since he didn't get a good look at me, he believed Edwin's act that I'd died."

She shuddered, and he chided himself for mentioning his death so casually.

"I'm sorry—"

"No, Marcus . . . I . . . *I'm* sorry." She wiped her face, but her tears didn't cease. "It's my fault he tried to . . . to . . ." She sobbed, and Marcus couldn't resist any longer. He wrapped his arms around her and held her while she cried.

After several moments, Adriana spoke quietly. "When my father returned home and announced he'd defeated your father, the first thing I did was ask him about you."

Relief flowed through him. She hadn't forgotten him.

"I think he'd forgotten about you, but he said you likely had died in your tower, as your father couldn't have been sending you supplies. I asked him to find you and bring you here, and that's when . . . that's when . . ."

Marcus rubbed her back and rested his cheek against her head, unsure what else to do. "That doesn't make it your fault—"

"He told me he'd arranged my marriage to Lord Thorne," Adriana burst out. "I told him I would never marry another man while there was even a chance you lived. He said he'd send someone to discover if you'd survived, but instead he sent someone to kill you. When I overheard the assassin giving his report, Father claimed it was because he feared you would rally any remnants of your family's supporters against us, that killing you was for the good of Aedyllan."

She shook her head, her voice small as she said, "I know it

was because of me. Marcus, I—"

"Hush, beloved, no." He tightened his hold on her, as if he could squeeze his reassurance into her. "Thank you for asking for me. You couldn't have guessed that's how he would react, and you didn't send that assassin. That wasn't your doing."

She sniffled. "I'm so glad you're alive. But . . . why are you here? There's nowhere more dangerous for you. If Father discovers you—"

"He won't recognize me. Besides, he believes I'm dead."

"Is Edwin still with you?"

"Yes. I'd . . ." He stopped himself before saying he'd have died at the knight's hands, if not for Edwin. "I'm not sure how I would have handled the last week without him."

"Good. I always liked him." She curled tighter against him. "Where are you staying?"

"Erm . . ." This was the complicated, embarrassing part. "Downstairs."

Adriana shifted out of his arms so she could meet his eyes. "Downstairs? What does that mean?"

"On the ground floor of your father's castle." He scratched at the side of his neck as he struggled to force the words out of his mouth. "With the . . . other servants."

CHAPTER 12

Adriana stared at Marcus, her confusion mounting. Perhaps it was her exhaustion from poor sleep and being awoken in the middle of the night, or perhaps it was due to the riot of emotions sparked by finding Marcus alive and in her room. Either way, she couldn't comprehend what he was saying.

"Other . . . servants?" she repeated.

Marcus's posture drooped as he angled away from her. "What is a prince without a crown, without a family, without a home, without even a copper piece to his name? I headed to Glenborough because I needed to know that you, at least, were alive and well. After I heard you were about to be wed to a wealthy lord who can provide for you and whose coffers will help stabilize Aedyllan . . . There wasn't any reason to stay. Edwin and I had run out of anything valuable to trade for food and lodging, and there were few jobs available. So when we received an offer of employment from a nobleman who doesn't live near Faine Castle, we accepted. Even though this noble-man makes his servants sign contracts agreeing to serve for five years or pay a large severance debt." His shoulders hunched. "We saw it as a guarantee of food and shelter for five years. I didn't expect him to come here."

Sorrow for the loneliness, grief, and uncertainty Marcus must have experienced after emerging from his tower momentarily distracted Adriana from what he'd implied. Then it hit her, like a branch of snow dumped on her head.

"You're serving *Lord Thorne*?"

"Yes. I'm . . ." He slumped further. "A lowly servant to your betrothed."

Adriana didn't know what to say. He looked so ashamed when he had no right to be. He'd tried to start a new life despite how wrong everything had gone, and things had only become worse. Although it hurt to know he hadn't originally intended to come for her, she couldn't really blame him. He had no title, no home, no fortune, and he'd learned she was about to be married to someone who did have those things, with no way of knowing she still wanted *him*, not some rich nobleman she'd never met. And his comment about Aedyllan's stability . . . even when he was heartbroken, he still was thinking of peace, and it both made her love him more and cracked her heart in two.

Before she could organize her thoughts, Marcus straightened, some of his princely bearing returning as he faced her again.

"Selfishly, I'm glad, though, because it means I can see you." He brushed his fingertips over her jawline. "Tell me honestly—did you agree to marry him?"

His fingers left her skin, but she caught his hand and pressed his palm to her cheek. "No. But my father won't relent."

Anger flashed through his eyes. "I didn't think your father would do that to you."

There was a time she also had believed Father would accept her refusal. "The war hardened him. He's determined to see this marriage happen, no matter what I say or even what Jairus says."

"I see," Marcus whispered. "Will you be all right?"

"All right?" She tightened her grip on his hand against her cheek. "Do you think it wouldn't torture me to see the man I love every day while married to another?"

"Love?" Marcus choked out. He raised his other palm to her cheek and leaned closer, cradling her face in a way that made her breath catch. "Still? Even though I'm penniless and trapped in servitude?"

Adriana released his hand to stroke his lengthy dark hair. It wasn't nearly as silky-soft as she remembered it being, but she didn't care. "Don't you still love me?"

"I could never stop loving you." Passion flooded those simple words as he rested his forehead against hers.

"Then why do you doubt me?" she said softly.

Tentatively, she shifted and tilted her face, bringing her

lips to his, but she didn't kiss him, waiting for him to make the next move.

"Adriana . . ." Marcus breathed against her mouth.

Then his lips pressed into hers, gently at first, but with increasing desperation. She returned the kiss, pouring in every moment of missing him and dreaming of their reunion for the last four years. Everything else faded away, and in that moment, it was only them, their breath intermingling and their arms around each other, holding each other close as if they had no intention of ever being separated.

But through the euphoria, a distant part of Adriana's mind called a warning. This couldn't be—not yet.

Marcus must have had a similar thought, because they both broke away and subtly eased back at the same time.

"I'm sorry," he panted. "That wasn't—I shouldn't have . . ."

She couldn't help a small chuckle. "It takes two to kiss." She placed a quick peck on his cheek. "I've missed kissing you, beloved."

Marcus groaned. "Adriana . . . I have nothing to offer you. I can only break the contract I signed if I pay Lord Thorne one hundred gold, and—"

"One hundred gold?" Surely she'd misheard him.

He nodded grimly. "And one hundred more for Edwin, who I obviously won't leave behind. We'll have to hide from Thorne, because if we're ever caught, he could drag us back.

Or possibly throw us in prison. Maybe worse, I don't know. And I can't even guarantee you shelter from the snow. I can't ask you to accept that."

Her mind whirled. There was no chance she could get her hands on two hundred gold. Father would have to withdraw that much from the treasury himself, and when he was already worried the royal coffers were too low, he would never agree. Especially not to help a man he'd tried to kill.

"Why did you accept such horrible terms?" The moment the question spilled out, she wished she could take it back.

"It seemed better than being homeless," Marcus whispered with a shrug.

"I'm sorry." She shook her head. "Perhaps we could leave Aedyllan entirely—"

"Adriana." The soft, sad tone made her freeze. "Aside from the dangers of running away without money in winter, what conflict might an Alimer stealing you away from your wedding stir up?"

Her lower lip trembled. If it was only the king's treasury as a concern, she could brush that aside. Father could find a bride for Jairus instead of forcing Adriana to wed the first lout with a fat purse who made an offer. But Marcus had a point. If Father realized whom she had run away with, it would verify his belief that Marcus was a threat to his rule.

"Perhaps there's another way," she said slowly. "We just

need to stop the wedding. That will buy us time to solve our other problems."

Marcus looked doubtful. "But you said your father—"

"There *must* be a way." She tapped a finger against her lips. "We'll figure out something. In the meantime, I'll warn Leena that you're both here. She won't tell a soul. Jairus only met you once and Father scarcely paid you any heed, so you're probably right that they won't recognize you. That gives us two and a half days to convince my father to call off the wedding."

"What if you'd be better off with him?" Agony reflected in his eyes. "I'm nothing—"

"I don't care!" She cupped his face in her hands, fighting tears yet again. "I want *you.* It's always been you. I'd rather be a pauper with you than a princess with him. I've waited so long. Please don't give up on the dream of us now."

A pained look crossed his countenance. "I'm sorry I didn't fight harder for our dream—or fight at all. I let you down—"

"What are you talking about?"

He pulled her hands down and stared out the window. "What did I do to make our dreams a reality for the year and a half we secretly courted? So many things I didn't try because I was afraid of my father or because it was easy to believe it wouldn't work. I fixated on the ways things could go wrong, or I stupidly waited for others to change their minds instead of acting. I could make a list of all the things I talked myself out of attempting, but it won't change that I didn't do them when it mattered."

Adriana bit the inside of her cheek. She'd had similar thoughts over the last few years about her own complacency.

"Maybe my brothers were right," he murmured. "I was foolish and naïve and noncommittal—although they were wrong about what action to take. I should have taken risks for my dreams. How can I say that peace and marriage to you was my goal while I did nothing but hide, wait, and hope? And now I'm doing it again, aren't I? Finding reasons to give up before we've even tried."

She hesitated, searching for the right response. "First, I don't think anything we could have done would have changed this outcome. The princes were too greedy and stubborn—"

"That doesn't mean I shouldn't have tried. I failed you. I failed all of Aedyllan."

"Marcus." She laid a hand on his forearm. "Listen to me. Maybe there was more we could have or should have done. I've spent so much time wishing I'd been bolder or had known the perfect argument to make to avoid your imprisonment, the war, and my father sending that assassin. Perhaps we were young and short-sighted and didn't live like we had any power to pursue our dreams. It's also wise to think about possible repercussions and not rush into foolish actions—that isn't the same as not acting at all. But we can't let the weight of could haves and unprovable hypotheticals steal our lives and choices now."

Marcus lifted his head. His jaw set as his shoulders drew back in silent resolve and determination glinted in the depths of his brown eyes. "You're right. We can learn from our inaction and do better. I'll help you avoid this marriage. Maybe stopping the wedding won't let me marry you—"

"But it's a step in that direction." Her heart gave a little twirl. She shifted to sit next to him on the edge of the bed, wrapped an arm around his waist, and leaned her head on his shoulder. "It gives us a chance."

CHAPTER 13

Marcus hadn't fully dared to hope that Adriana would want to find a way back to a shared future. He had made her so many broken promises. In the past, he'd failed to work toward peace as he'd desired and failed to protect his father's subjects, earning their derision. How could he fail the woman he loved, too?

Hopes and dreams without action were empty. He no longer wanted to wait without taking steps to make his dreams a reality.

"I'm sorry it took me so long to realize wanting something isn't enough if I don't take risks to pursue it," Marcus whispered. He reached over and clasped her hand, weaving their fingers together. Her hands were so tiny compared to his. "I can't guarantee anything, so I won't make promises I may not be able to keep. But I do promise you that I will do more than hope for us—I'll fight for us."

Even if he wasn't entirely certain how to do that yet.

"That's all I ask," Adriana replied, the love in her gaze

making his heart soar. "But let's be cautious. Don't put yourself in danger unnecessarily. We could . . . hm . . ." She straightened so abruptly her head bumped against the side of his jaw, and he barely held back a yelp. "Wait! You're serving my betrothed."

He winced. "Yes?"

"Something about him unsettles me, and the unjust terms of his contract make me question his integrity. You'll be around him, can speak with his servants, and have access to his rooms. Maybe *you* can discover if he has any reputation-destroying secrets."

"I will attempt to search his room tomorrow. I don't suppose the unfair contract itself would be enough for your father?"

Adriana sighed. "No. As long as the contracts are legal, my father won't care that they're unfair—he wants this marriage too badly."

Wondering if she was silently judging him for being so foolish as to sign the contract, Marcus nodded. He'd been so desperate for a way to leave before Adriana's wedding . . . If anything, that made it worse. How could he have believed she was willing to marry another?

"I'd hoped you were happy," he said abruptly, needing her to understand. "When I accepted this employment, that is. I didn't know you didn't want this—"

"I know." She gave an abashed smile. "Four years ago, the

news from Alimer Principality was jumbled. Initially, it was reported you were soon to be married. I refused to believe it. If it had been true, I wouldn't have wanted to hear your name again. Then the true news came, including the fae curse on the tower. That was the only thing that stopped me from trying to rescue you myself." She laughed softly. "I don't blame you for thinking I'd moved on—even if I am a little hurt you believed I'd forget you so easily. I thought of you so often . . . oh!"

Adriana leapt up. "I wrote to you, but Father wouldn't let me send the letters. Prince Arlius had forbidden anyone from approaching the tower without his consent. I kept writing anyway, hoping someday I could get them to you."

Curious, Marcus followed her to the wardrobe. She dug out a velvet sack from behind her gowns and turned around, almost running into his chest. He looked from the wardrobe to her hazel eyes with a soft smile.

"I remember hiding in there," he said fondly. "And falling out."

By the way a blush spread up her throat to her ears, she remembered, too.

"I also remember wishing we didn't have to hide." His smile fell.

"After we ruin this wedding, we will find a way to be together. Preferably without hiding." Adriana held out the bag, and Marcus accepted it from her.

Less than three days didn't seem like enough time to stop a wedding mandated by a king, but they'd find a solution. He would do whatever it took.

Marcus pulled open the drawstring on the bag, revealing a mound of folded letters. Emotion tightened his throat. "You kept them after you thought I was . . . gone?"

"Of course I did."

"I saved all the letters I wrote to you, too, but there's not this many. My father refused to send more parchment." He ducked his head. "I'm afraid I left them in the tower. But . . . I reread them so many times I have most of them memorized."

"Really?" She dragged him back to the bed. After they were sitting with their backs against the curtain covering the wall, she snuggled against his side. "Would you recite one of your letters to me? Please?"

Marcus shifted to wrap his arm around her shoulders. "All right." He took a deep breath and closed his eyes before beginning.

"*Dear Adriana,*

I've been in this tower for three months. Only just over three months since last I saw you, but it feels like an eternity. A part of my soul is missing without you.

The moon is full and bright tonight, and as I look at it, I wonder if you're looking, too. If I could send my love to the moon so you could feel my dedication to you in a moonbeam, I would.

Do you remember that day last winter when we stayed out too late, and I rode with you almost to your castle? The moonlight bounced off the snow, creating a perpetual twilight. It was like riding through a dream, all the more so because you were beside me.

Keep holding your hope for the dream of us like a bright candle in your heart, the way you did for the last year and a half.

With all of my love,

Your Marcus"

He finished reciting the letter and opened his eyes. Adriana had closed her own eyes, tucked her arm around his waist, and pressed closer against him. He wished they could stay like that forever, but she looked sleepy.

As if in confirmation, she yawned.

"As much as I'd love to sit with you all night," Marcus said, "I should sleep in case Lord Thorne calls on me to serve him tomorrow." He wasn't even sure what that might look like.

"And I'm supposed to spend most of tomorrow with him." She wrinkled her nose. "I suppose if we want to appear unsuspicious while we plot, we should both rest."

"Agreed." But he couldn't seem to make himself move.

Adriana craned her neck back to look up at him. "You were given a tour, right? Do you know where the sitting room is on the ground floor?"

He nodded.

"Meet me there tomorrow night after the ninth hour."

"I'll be there," he promised. At last, he made himself release her shoulders and move, but Adriana gripped his tunic.

"Please be careful climbing down. I can't lose you again."

The ice and snow on the trellis did worry him a little, but he grinned. "I've climbed that wall many times. I'll be fine." He covered her fist against his chest as he leaned closer. "And I already promised I'd see you tomorrow night."

She smiled, a bit of color creeping into her cheeks as she pulled her hand out from under his. "You should go before I give in to the desire to kiss you again."

That rather made Marcus want to stay, but Adriana was right. They both needed to sleep—and Edwin would be going mad with worry over his delay in returning.

"I love you." Marcus brushed a kiss against her forehead.

"I love you," she murmured.

And then, before he could lose his willpower, Marcus went to the window, clenched the bag of letters in his teeth, and climbed down the trellis.

Edwin looked equal parts relieved and like he was considering killing Marcus himself when Marcus crept back into the servants' room.

He listened with a pinched expression to Marcus's explanation of their plan to stop the wedding, then was silent for several heartbeats. At last, he sighed.

"I suspected this is where we'd end up the moment you decided to sneak up there." Edwin shook his head. "But I'm not leaving you to face this alone. Between the two of us, we have a greater chance of discovering a reason why Lord Thorne won't make a suitable husband and son-in-law."

Tension drained from Marcus's shoulders. He hadn't realized how afraid he was that Edwin would be angry or would want to make his escape alone. "You're a far better friend than I deserve."

"I'm also your only friend," Edwin quipped.

Marcus snorted. "I don't see you having any other friends, either."

"Unfortunately," Edwin said, donning a melodramatically sorrowful expression, "I was imprisoned for years and had no opportunity to build friendships."

Marcus stifled a snort and gave his friend a gentle shove. "Now, if you don't mind, I'd like to read some letters."

"Shouldn't you sleep?"

As if he could sleep after kissing Adriana. But he did need rest. "I won't stay up too late."

Edwin huffed and got off Marcus's narrow bed. "I suppose that means you're keeping that candle lit, then."

"Obviously."

"If I'm exhausted tomorrow, I'm blaming you."

Marcus made a face at Edwin, then withdrew a letter from the sack.

He read until his eyelids grew heavy. Adriana's letters were full of her life and heart—telling him about visits to the fluffy cows and annoyance with a prank Jairus had pulled, about good days and bad days. Like his own letters back in the tower, there were also memories of their secret rendezvous and lines about how much she missed and loved him.

It was one thing to be stuck in the tower thinking of Adriana and imagining that she was thinking of him, too. It was something else to know that all that time, she truly had been remembering him just as often as he had been missing her.

After hiding the letters inside his mattress, he blew out the candle and went to sleep with a lightness in his chest despite the uncertainty of the coming days.

CHAPTER 14

Adriana awoke with a smile on her face. Ignoring the chill, she went to the window, tossed open the shutters, and leaned out, inhaling a deep breath of the crisp morning air. Her skin prickled in response to the cold, but she didn't mind—it was a reminder of how alive she was, and how wonderfully alive Marcus was. For the first time in days, she wasn't wavering between unfeeling numbness and the urge to weep. She smiled down at the trellis. Hopefully no one would question how snow had been knocked off the iron bars.

The door to her chamber opened.

"Your Highness?" Leena sounded shocked. Of course she was, considering recently Adriana's handmaiden had nearly had to drag her out of bed.

With a wide grin, Adriana closed the shutters and hurried over to Leena. Seizing Leena's hand, she dragged her maid and friend over to sit on her bed.

"You seem . . . optimistic this morning," Leena said, but her face conveyed her skepticism.

"Leena." Adriana kept her voice low. "I have the best news." She paused, reflecting. "Well, maybe not *best*, as the situation is somewhat of a mess, but that's all right. Leena." She squeezed Leena's hand. "Marcus is alive."

Leena blinked, then a look of pity slipped over her features. "Your Highness—"

"No, it's true!" She winced at her own exclamation and leaned closer, lowering her voice. "He's here, in the castle. He survived, and Edwin faked Marcus's death, and they traveled to Glenborough for me but heard I was about to be married, so they sought employment; but oh, Leena. You'll never guess who hired them as servants. Lord Thorne!"

"What?" Leena shook her head. "That . . . that isn't possible. Is it?"

Adriana nodded enthusiastically. "Marcus climbed the trellis last night and told me everything. Don't look at me like that. I didn't dream it." She tugged Leena over to the window and reopened the shutters. "Look."

With an unconvinced frown, Leena peered over the sill, then gasped and slammed the shutters closed, her eyes wide. "Something has been climbing on the trellis . . . it was really Prince Marcus? Truly?"

"Yes!" Adriana clapped a hand over her mouth.

"Although I suppose he isn't strictly a prince anymore . . . and wait, you say he's serving Lord Thorne?" Leena's smile faded. "Oh. Oh, no; that is a mess."

Adriana drifted over to her desk and slumped into the chair. "It is. Marcus and Edwin can't even quit because of the unfair contract Lucien made them sign. So we can't let anyone know who they are. If you see them, you don't recognize them."

Leena nodded dazedly.

"Second, we need to stop the wedding."

"Even your brother couldn't manage that."

"I know." Adriana nibbled at her lower lip. "I'm hoping Marcus and Edwin can find evidence that Lord Thorne isn't a good man, but we should think about other options as well."

As she went about stoking the fire back up, Leena asked, "Why don't you just run away?"

"I'd like to." With a sigh, Adriana rested her chin in her hand. "But neither of us have any money, and running away in the middle of winter with no long-term plan, nowhere to run to, and when Father and Lucien would both want to hunt us down . . ." There was a chance it would end with Marcus's real death. "Not to mention it might destroy the peace Father fought for. It's best we find another way."

Leena opened the wardrobe, then peered over at Adriana. "Then . . . are you meeting with Lord Thorne as planned, Your Highness?"

Wincing, Adriana nodded. She rose from the table and joined Leena. "I'm thinking the green linen with the bronze belt. It's plain enough that it doesn't appear I'm eager to impress, but rich enough that Father won't accuse me of purposefully looking too plain."

"A wise choice."

Leena helped Adriana don the gown. Made from thick, tightly knit linen, the dark-green dress was soft and decently warm. It was a simple style with a high, rounded neckline and long sleeves, embellished with a gold-embroidered violet ribbon that covered the sleeves' seams and trimmed the collar and cuffs.

They added a belt of interlocking bronze circles over her hips, then Leena gently ran a wide-toothed comb through Adriana's hair. If she hadn't thrashed about thinking she was being attacked last night—and then been kissed rather passionately—she would have simply undone the plait she'd woven before bed, but her hair was noticeably tangled. Unfortunately, despite how frequently Leena rewet the comb, Adriana's curls were wild and frizzy by the time Leena was done.

She frowned at the mirror, then shrugged. "I don't care about impressing Lucien, anyway." Standing, she took a steadying breath. "Wish me luck. And remember, if you encounter Marcus or Edwin—"

"I've never seen them before." Leena gave a small curtsy. "I hope today goes well, Your Highness. Or poorly, as the case may be."

Adriana laughed. "True. Perhaps we should wish that today is so disastrous Father chases Lord Thorne out of the castle."

An improbable hope, but when had she ever let that stop her from dreaming?

———

Breakfast, thankfully, was in the great hall. So while Adriana had to cope with sitting next to Lucien Thorne and politely listening to him talk about his wealth and lands—recently expanded by a grant from her father—and fighting and hunting, at least it was in a busy area. Lucien sat to Father's left, with Jairus to Father's right, and often Jairus and Father spoke to her betrothed so she didn't have to. In fact, she suspected Jairus was purposefully asking questions to give her a reprieve from pretending to care.

She kept scanning the hall, looking for Marcus or Edwin. They didn't appear, which made sense. The castle's servants were busy serving the royal family and the knights and their families, including the knights Lucien had brought with him. Lucien's servants would only be in the way if they attempted to insert themselves into Faine Castle's day-to-day life.

As Lucien leaned forward a little to peer around Father at Jairus, Adriana noted that he was wearing the silver hair stick again. Men's hair sticks had fallen out of style in the last decade, and his wasn't particularly notable other than being silver. Maybe he wore it because it was the closest a nonroyal was allowed to get to wearing a crown. He did give her the impression he liked to show off.

After breakfast, Jairus surprised her by standing and turning to Lucien. "Lord Lucien. I'd very much like to see this military prowess in person. I regret that my duties as my father's heir and the defender of Faine Castle kept me away from the battlefield, so I missed the chance to observe you. Perhaps we could have a friendly competition? Archery and spear tosses, perhaps, as I'd hate to injure my sister's groom days before her wedding."

Father cast a dark look at Jairus. For her part, Adriana could have hugged her brother.

"That's a wonderful idea!" Adriana smiled brightly and lightly touched the back of Lucien's hand. "I'd love to observe you both. It sounds thrilling." It sounded cold and boring, but it meant Lucien's primary attention wouldn't be on her for a while.

Her touch must have had the desired effect, because Lucien puffed out his chest and tossed his head, his brown hair sliding over his shoulders. "Of course. It would be my honor to practice with my crown prince, and if my wife wishes to see me in action, I can hardly refuse her."

Her smile almost wavered at *my wife*, but somehow, she kept her composure. "Excellent! Why don't we fetch some warmer attire and then meet near the stables?"

Father glared at her, but she ignored him as she left the table, already headed to her room. She took her time putting on a warm pair of long woolen stockings, thick boots, mittens, and a fur-lined cloak with a hood, and dallied on the stairs. No reason to spend one moment more with her unwanted betrothed than necessary.

Unfortunately, Lucien had insisted on waiting for her, so Jairus, Lucien, and several servants were standing in the great hall when she arrived. She plastered on a smile, but when her gaze fell on Marcus, standing off to the side behind Lucien and holding a bow and quiver, her smile became real. She quickly snapped her attention back to Lucien before anyone could catch her looking at the wrong man.

"Shall we?" Lucien offered her his arm.

Clenching her teeth, Adriana wrapped her mittened hand around the crook of his elbow.

Jairus led the way as they crunched through the snow. Thankfully, the entrance to the castle was on the opposite side from her bedroom, so they went around the nearer end of the castle and didn't pass by the trellis. They wound around the stone building that housed the stables, chicken coop, and goat pen. Other servants were already setting up two large targets made of straw-stuffed squares of hemp fabric painted with red circles.

While Jairus and Lucien debated distances and angles on

the slight incline of the hill, Adriana fought to keep from glancing at Marcus. He stood with a middle-aged man she didn't recognize, likely another of Lucien's servants. But Marcus looked so handsome, it was difficult not to watch him from the corner of her eye.

He wore a simple, red tunic that didn't reach his knees over woolen trousers. The tunic must have been borrowed, because the length seemed short even for a servant, and it pulled a little across his chest. His shoulders looked broad and strong beneath his gray cloak, and the belt only emphasized his lean but athletic build. He'd certainly kept up his physique despite being locked in a tower. Or perhaps keeping up his training was one of the few things he could do while incarcerated.

Although Marcus had done the top half of his hair with only one simple braid on each side of his head, they were still perfectly neat. A light breeze tousled the ends of his black hair, and she turned away before she got distracted by thoughts of running her fingers through that hair.

No, she needed to ignore him. If she were caught mooning over Marcus before they had a plan in place, any chance they had of being together would be lost.

"Acceptable?" Jairus said, finishing some discussion she hadn't been listening to.

Lucien nodded. "After you, Your Highness."

Jairus's personal servant, Felix, rushed to hand Jairus his

bow and an arrow. Then Felix stepped back, holding the quiver for her brother.

Jairus nocked his arrow and moved into position, adjusting his footing in the snow. In one swift motion, he raised and drew the bow, and in the space of a breath, loosed the arrow. The shaft arced through the air before landing in the center red circle, almost in the dead center of his target. Adriana grinned and clapped her hands, although it didn't make much sound through her mittens.

"Outstanding, Prince Jairus." Had she imagined a sharp edge to Lucien's tone?

Felix offered another arrow. Soon, three arrows were clustered near the center of Jairus's target.

"It's truly a shame you couldn't have joined us on the battlefield." That time Adriana was certain she hadn't imagined the mocking, irritated note to her betrothed's words. "I suppose not all of us are fortunate enough to prove our worth and claim glory in battle." The close-lipped smile he gave her brother had a condescending twist to it.

Adriana stifled a frown. A memory came back to her, of a warm spring day as she gleefully stroked a fluffy calf that was only twelve days old while the cowherd checked on its mother. The visit to the cattle had partly been a cover to see Marcus, and he'd been sitting beside her.

As Marcus had watched the cattle, he'd leaned back on his

hands and said, "Isn't life far more valuable than death? Those who quietly and passionately care for life, like that cowherd, have done something important. Aren't they at least as worthy of praise as a knight whose claim to glory is how many lives he's ended? If it is done in defense, to protect lives, I understand. It's why I learned to fight at all. But why can't my father see the value in nurturing life and peace instead of craving more power at the cost of bloodshed?"

Adriana didn't think Marcus had any idea how attractive he was when he showed his soft heart.

She was certain that Lucien was oblivious to how completely unattractive she found his boasts of battle and death.

Marcus silently slipped forward and held forth the bow and an arrow. Lucien accepted them with scarcely a glance at Marcus, who bowed his head and shifted out of his lord's way. It was unsettling to watch a man she had known as a prince be so subservient, but she didn't see a hint of resentment or discomfort on his face. Marcus had never held his crown or his pride that dear—other than having a burden of caring for his subjects.

Lucien took a moment longer to aim than Jairus had, but his less flashy style had its merits. His arrow buried itself in the exact center of his target. A satisfied smirk flitted across his face before his features smoothed. Adriana forced herself to applaud.

"Your abilities truly weren't exaggerated," Jairus noted, his tone friendly.

As Lucien took another arrow from Marcus, he looked over at Adriana. "I assure you, my performance is always exemplary." He winked at her before turning back to his target.

Was that meant to be flirting? It wasn't particularly effective flirting. She wasn't certain if he was boasting about his archery or his strength in general, or if it was supposed to be an innuendo. Her stomach churned. Hopefully he simply believed she'd swoon over his archery prowess.

Admittedly, his archery skills were impressive. Lucien's arrows were grouped together more tightly than Jairus's and closer to the center. Felix and Marcus jogged across the distance to retrieve the arrows. As they returned, Marcus's gaze darted over to her for a moment, but his expression betrayed nothing.

Two more rounds of archery had much the same results—Jairus released quickly and landed his arrows in the center of the target, but Lucien's arrows buried deeper and with even greater accuracy. Once he split the edge of one of his previous arrows, and his smug countenance made her want to roll her eyes, but she refrained.

After that, another servant brought out spears. Adriana pulled her hood tighter about her head and wrapped her arms around her middle, but she didn't say that she was cold. As soon as they went inside, entertaining Lucien would fall on her, and she wanted to avoid that for as long as possible.

Both men threw the spears, landing equally accurate strikes. Marcus and Felix ran to collect the spears, Marcus moving quicker and yanking out the spear with ease.

"Your servant carries himself well," Jairus said as Marcus returned. "He holds that spear like he knows what to do with it. I could almost mistake him for a knight or a nobleman."

Lucien stood a little taller. "I employ only the very best. Such strong, handsome, capable, and well-mannered young men as Marcus Williams and his brother make excellent additions to my retinue. Like all of my servants, he is dedicated, obedient, and loyal. Naturally, he understands what an honor it is to serve me. Isn't that right, Williams?"

Marcus bowed. "Yes, my lord. I'm honored and grateful for your beneficence in giving me a place in your household."

Jairus nodded, clearly impressed, while Adriana's stomach roiled.

"Observe." Lucien snatched the spear from Marcus. "My feet are getting chilled in this snow. Williams, dry my boots with your cloak."

With a soft "yes, my lord," Marcus bowed and pulled off his cloak. His broad shoulders strained against his tunic as he knelt in the snow, wiping muck off one of Lucien's boots and then the other. Adriana bit her tongue. It was not her place to tell a man what he could or could not order his own servant to do, especially not as a woman. And while his order was cold-hearted and debasing, it wasn't heinous. She couldn't risk letting on that she cared about Marcus and already hated Lucien by demanding he stop.

"Leave the cloak for me to stand on," Lucien ordered as Marcus began to rise.

"Of course, my lord." His eyes downcast, Marcus spread his cloak over the tramped-down snow and withdrew behind Lucien. Melting snow left wet spots on his trousers, and his tunic didn't look very warm.

Adriana squeezed herself tighter, feeling ill as she put the pieces together. Lucien hadn't picked Marcus to attend him at random. He didn't know who Marcus was or who he was to her, but his choice of servant was calculated. Marcus was tall, attractive, and strong with a hint of physical prowess, and he spoke and moved with the grace and poise of a nobleman. Lucien had wanted Marcus to wait on him for the same reason a man might collar a gryphon or make a cloak from the skin of a great bear—to make himself appear more remarkable for mastering another living thing that was itself impressive.

He had trotted out Marcus like a prized exotic pet.

If only that would be enough to convince Father that Lord Lucien wasn't a worthy husband. Father would probably claim it was natural for a man to strive to impress his future bride and brother-in-law by picking his best servants. He might not interpret it as using another human as an accessory and treating them as less than human. But she did, and even if the servant in question hadn't been Marcus, Lucien's behavior would have repulsed her.

Jairus, too, appeared uncomfortable as he glanced between Lucien standing on Marcus's dirty cloak and Marcus standing with his head bowed. He took his spear from Felix and cleared his throat. "Shall we?"

CHAPTER 15

Marcus jogged across the snow to retrieve the spear for the third time, ignoring how cold his wet trousers were and how the air nipped through his tunic and undershirt without the added protection of his cloak.

He'd known Lord Thorne was up to something when he'd stomped into the servants' room after breakfast and barked at them to line up. After scrutinizing them, he'd ordered Roger to step forward—"because you've served me the longest"—and then Marcus.

"You possess the strongest and most refined appearance. You'll hold my weapons and retrieve them from the target for me," Lord Thorne had said. "You will be the picture of a meek servant, moving quickly and quietly, speaking only when spoken to, and immediately following any command with utmost deference. Convince me that you love serving me. If you don't . . . well. I'd rather not have to discipline you."

Marcus had agreed, but he'd also noted the looks the others had sent his way. Most of the servants had looked worried, frightened even. But Roger had appeared relieved, almost smug, as if glad his lord's focus would be on someone other than himself.

Thorne claiming Marcus's cloak for his dirty boots hadn't been what Marcus expected, although he hadn't been sure what to expect. Perhaps finding fault with Lord Lucien Thorne wouldn't be difficult after all. Unfortunately, as humiliating as that had been, King Mortimer likely wouldn't find bullying a servant worth withdrawing from a wedding that would refill the treasury and make his rule more secure.

"Your servant appears cold," Prince Jairus noted. His eyes held a touch of sympathy as he watched Marcus return with the spear. "Perhaps we should retire inside."

"Before we've determined a winner of our friendly contest?" Thorne flashed a cocky grin. "Worried you'll lose again?"

Jairus frowned. "The outcome of the match wasn't the point and doesn't concern me. Does the welfare of your servant not concern you?"

Marcus forced himself not to react. Although he'd met Jairus only briefly at the hunt where he'd first met Adriana, she'd told him about her brother. It seemed he was worthy of the admiration given him by his little sister.

"Of course. If he's too chilled, we can abandon our tie-breaking throw." Thorne turned his steely gaze on Marcus, and there was a warning in that look.

"I'm all right, my lord and Your Highness. The activity has kept me warm."

"However, I'm cold," Adriana said. She took a couple steps closer from where she had been watching in silence. "My nose and feet would be grateful for a fire."

It took a great deal of effort for Marcus not to turn to look at her.

Thorne gave her an indulgent smile. "I certainly won't allow my bride to freeze. Come, let's return inside." He glanced at Marcus. "Williams. Help the king's servants put away the targets and spears. Then return my bow and quiver to my quarters and dress in dry garments."

Marcus bowed, fighting a shiver. "Yes, my lord."

"Lucien," Adriana said as she glided over to his side. Her smile was tight and forced. "My family's servants are very efficient and don't require extra help. I'm afraid Williams may only get in the way and frustrate them."

To Marcus's relief, Thorne nodded. "True enough. Follow along with my bow and quiver, then, Williams."

"Yes, my lord." That time, Marcus couldn't stop the shiver.

Once inside, Thorne, Adriana, and Jairus headed for the sitting room. At least Jairus would be there for Adriana. Marcus delivered Thorne's bow to his room. He hesitated, looking around the chamber. This was an opportunity to search Thorne's belongings for anything incriminating. But did he dare rifle through his lord's personal things?

He decided to do so, but very carefully, disrupting the room as little as possible and returning everything to exactly how he'd found it. That meant he couldn't fully dig through Thorne's trunks. From what he could see, two trunks were full of clothing and personal care items such as perfumes, scented bath salts, and hair oils. Marcus lingered for a moment over the oils. Oh, how he missed hair oils and scented baths and other luxuries he'd not used since before his incarceration.

The final trunk held bags of coins, which were likely the bride price. He wrinkled his nose as he closed that trunk. Nobles married off their children for various advantages all the time, just as his own father had tried to marry him off to secure military support. But he disliked the practice, and he liked it even less when it felt like Lucien Thorne was buying Adriana.

Unfortunately, he found nothing that would incriminate Lucien in front of the king. Perhaps there was something buried at the bottom of one of the trunks, but there was no way he could pull everything out without it being obvious someone had gone through them. Defeated, he returned to the room he shared with the other servants. His wet cloak, which was draped over his left arm, was making his chill worse rather than better, and he was ready to change into dry trousers.

Edwin jolted to his feet when Marcus entered and scrutinized him from head to foot. "Did you fall in the snow?"

Marcus shook his head. "Lord Thorne . . . required my cloak to clean his boots."

"What?" Edwin's expression darkened like a storm cloud. "I should have known a man who wrote a contract like that would be a churl."

"Never let him hear you say that," a lanky servant named Jacob said from where he lounged on his bed near the fire. "Most of the time, Lord Thorne's decent enough. But he enjoys using his power as our lord and the holder of contracts he knows we can't afford to break to humiliate us. If he's in a particularly bad mood, he gets violent. Disobedience or disrespecting him are quick ways to put him in a bad mood."

Pulling off his boots, Marcus sighed. "I'm sorry, Ed. I shouldn't have been so eager to take the first position that came our way." Although such testimony from Thorne's servants might work in his and Adriana's favor.

Edwin flopped on his own bed. "I was just as stupid, if not worse. I ignored my instincts and agreed. After all, if I'd told you no, you wouldn't have signed. Even if I'd said no and you still signed, no one forced me to join you."

"I still feel like this is my fault—"

"You aren't supposed to carry responsibility for everything in Aedyllan, you know." Edwin rolled his eyes.

Marcus didn't argue. He knew it was true, but that didn't change the fact that if Thorne ever directed his pettiness or hostility toward Edwin, Marcus would feel responsible.

He pulled on a clean pair of trousers—another borrowed pair, as Edwin had washed their clothing while Marcus was out, and everything was still wet. The trousers were rough and a touch short, but they were dry. Then he stood by the fire to finish warming up and dry where the snow on the cloak had seeped into his overtunic.

"Where are the others?"

"Doing more washing of Lord Thorne's and the knights' clothing," Jacob said. "Edwin and I are stuck here in case Lord Thorne requires more servants for anything. Doubt it, though, as the Faines' servants have things well in hand."

Marcus nodded. That might leave the rest of the day to kill. Ugh, he'd thought he was done being trapped in a stone building with nothing to do.

"You fight at all, Jacob?"

The young man blinked. "Erm, no?"

"Shame. Edwin and I haven't had a chance to practice with a new sparring partner in a while."

Jacob straightened, glancing back and forth between them. "What sparring do you do?"

"Wrestling," Edwin said. "Staff. Sword."

"We both used to be decent archers." Marcus recalled that morning's events with some resentment and bruised pride. "I haven't drawn a bow in far too long, though."

"I don't know what kind of masters you had that allowed such pursuits," Jacob said, shaking his head, "but I'd keep that to yourselves. I can't imagine Lord Thorne would take kindly to his servants partaking in a knight's pastimes. Or he'd decide you'd make good sparring partners, which would end horribly. Either he'll wallop you squarely or he'll beat you to ease his hurt pride if he doesn't."

Marcus hadn't considered that his martial ability might be suspicious or cause more problems. After all, Edwin had trained with him even before becoming his bodyguard, and Father had never objected.

Just when Marcus was finally warm again, the door opened and Roger peered inside.

"Mar—ah, there you are. Our lord commands that you fetch the large jar of wine bearing the stamp of a sea serpent on the wax seal from his chambers and wait on him and the prince and princess in the study on the first floor." Roger's smile had a cruel edge. "Be quick about it, boy."

The door shut and Roger was gone before Marcus could so much as say yes.

Jacob snorted. "Roger is the best at reading Lord Thorne, and also the best at deflecting his ire. Other than maybe Steward Talwen. Watch out for both of them. They'll gladly throw you under the carriage to save themselves."

Edwin sent Marcus a look that said *be careful*. At least they were already planning on getting away from Thorne. Unfortunately, the plan was more of a goal than an actual plan at the moment, but they had time. Only two days, but that was better than nothing.

Thankfully Marcus knew exactly where the wine jar was from his earlier snooping. When he arrived in the sitting room, a couple of serving women were entering in front of him, bearing covered trays. A male servant was already inside, placing goblets on the small, round table that Adriana, Jairus, and Thorne were seated around. Roger stood in the shadows in a corner, ready if called upon, but unobtrusive.

Marcus approached Thorne, forcing himself not to glance at Adriana, and bowed.

"Excellent!" Thorne smiled. "Stand aside for the moment, and after the food is served, you will serve the wine."

With another bow, Marcus withdrew. While the women set out plates of food, he broke the wax seal on the wine jar and worked out the stopper, then looked around.

The sitting room was slightly larger than Adriana's bedchamber. A dark-blue woven rug covered most of the stone floor, the walls were covered with wood paneling, and a faint scent of dried lavender permeated the room underneath the savory scents of the food the servants were setting out. Aside from the table and its four wood chairs, several upholstered chairs and a chaise were arranged around a fireplace with a marble façade. A wood bookshelf held an impressive number of leather-bound books, a large basket in the corner appeared to be full of embroidery supplies, and a lyre and a lute hung from hooks on the wall beside a tapestry of a shoreline. In addition to the snapping fire, candles in the many wall sconces provided light.

The serving women left the room, and the man who had set out the goblets slipped back near the door. Likely one of the Faines' servants, ready to fetch anything requested by the prince or princess.

At least Jairus was there. Since learning that Thorne was the kind of man who liked to lord his power over others and could be vindictive, Marcus particularly disliked the idea of Adriana being left alone with him.

Thorne looked to Marcus, and he hastened over to pour the wine.

CHAPTER 16

The venison stew with roots and herbs and the fresh bread rolls smelled divine, so Adriana focused on the food and utensils being placed in front of her and not on Marcus standing a couple of paces away. She had thought there could be no greater torment than being indefinitely separated from the man she loved, but it turned out that being in the same room as him while his life depended on her not acknowledging him was worse.

All fae blessings upon Jairus, though. He'd made the time they'd spent so far in the sitting room tolerable by keeping Lucien's attention. She'd mostly blocked out what Lucien said, smiling or nodding or acting impressed when it appeared appropriate. He seemed to love to hear himself talk, particularly to boast about himself. She never would have been happy married to him.

Now to find a way to convince Father to call off the wedding. Unfortunately, he'd already conveyed that her potential happiness, or lack thereof, was not a deciding factor.

The servants left with the trays, and Marcus approached the table with the wine. He poured a little of the vibrant red liquid into Lucien's goblet, and the lord gave it a quick inspection before nodding. Marcus served the wine to Lucien, then to Jairus, and finally he was standing at her side, so close she could have leaned against him. She stared at her stew and hoped her face didn't look as warm as it felt.

Thankfully Marcus poured quickly and slipped away from the table.

"You said this Williams hasn't been with you long?" Jairus inquired. "He seems skilled in his role."

"I lured him and his brother away from another lord," Lucien said, his tone conspiratorial. "Men understand a worthy leader when they see one."

Well, Adriana could add *liar* to the list of her betrothed's unsavory characteristics, but it'd need to be a far more consequential lie to draw Father's ire.

"Oh?" Jairus peered over at Marcus. "Who did you serve before?"

She held her breath. Since the others' focus was already on Marcus, she let herself look at him—and oh, the torment of seeing him standing there with his handsome face, alive and well, but still out of reach.

Marcus inclined his head. "I'd rather not be perceived as potentially insulting my previous liege, Your Highness."

Jairus laughed. "Tactful and honorable. I can see why you'd want such a servant for your own household."

"Now, don't get any ideas about stealing him from me," Lucien said with a chuckle. "I have no intention of letting him go."

"He's a person, not livestock," Adriana snapped. Lucien frowned at her, and she wished she hadn't spoken. But she had, and she couldn't back down now. "A servant is free to accept any employment he wishes, and a person can't be stolen."

Lucien shrugged. "He'd have to break his contract to leave, and I know he doesn't have the coin to pay the debt that would incur. I suppose someone could pay the contract-breaking fee for him"—he grinned savagely—"which on reflection, would be rather like buying him, so maybe he is livestock. But I don't plan on accepting such payment from anyone other than him, so he can't be bought."

She gaped at him. "That . . . that's just slavery. And you can't refuse to accept payment in line with a contract—"

"My dearest bride," Lucien interrupted, "are you trying to run my household for me already?" He reached over and patted her hand. "Don't worry your pretty little head. It's all perfectly legal and within my rights, and I'll continue running the household so my princess can fill her days with leisure. And bear and care for my sons, of course."

She snatched her hand away, then furiously bit into a roll.

Her cheeks flamed, and she didn't dare look over to see Marcus's reaction.

"This wine is excellent," Jairus said.

That was all Lucien needed to start on a spiel about the wine and how expensive it was to have it imported from across the sea, but she wasn't listening. The tender pieces of venison in the stew were suddenly difficult to swallow, and her stomach tightened as his words replayed in her mind. He planned to keep her out of his affairs? A pretty accessory he kept around his castle—and who bore him children? A shiver went down her spine.

If running away with Marcus was what it took to avoid that future, she'd do it despite the risks.

Jairus finished his goblet.

"Refill the crown prince's wine," Lucien called.

"I'm all right—"

"Nonsense. You may not get this opportunity again, and now that the seal has been broken, it won't keep as well."

Adriana watched Marcus from the corner of her eye as he moved past Lucien and refilled Jairus's goblet.

"And the princess." As Marcus moved to her side, Lucien peered across the table. "Adriana, you've hardly touched your wine."

"Don't make me drink it all," Jairus teased.

She forced a smile and took a sip. It was good wine, rich

without being overpowering, sweet, and with a subtle cherry flavor. "Thank you, Lucien. It's delicious."

"Good." He lifted his goblet in a demanding fashion, and Marcus scurried over to fill it. "I've another, smaller jar we can share on our wedding day before consummating our marriage." He smirked.

Marcus jolted mid-pour, and wine sloshed over the side of the goblet onto Lucien, and in his sudden panic to correct it, he jerked the jar back and it slipped from his hands onto the table. By some miracle, the ceramic jar didn't break, but more crimson liquid splashed out before Marcus snatched it up against his chest. His face red as a beetroot, Marcus shuffled back and doubled over in a bow.

"My apologies, my lord, for my clumsiness. I don't know what—"

"Silence!"

Lucien's hands curled into fists, his knuckles turning white. Slowly, he stood, his teeth clenched so tightly the muscles along his jawline and neck corded. Wine stained the lower half of his sage tunic and dripped off the edge of the table.

"Take off your tunic and clean this mess," Lucien said in a low voice.

Marcus immediately set the jug on the table and undid his belt. Adriana looked to Jairus, half because she would get too flustered if she watched Marcus undressing, and half because she desperately hoped he would protect this servant he knew nothing about. They could have called for rags, but Marcus was already wiping up the spilled wine with his tunic. Just for a moment she glanced at him, now wearing a thin white linen undershirt that made the muscles in his arms more obvious. A few curls of chest hair poked out of the vee-shaped collar. Feeling a blush creeping up her neck, she turned back to Jairus.

Her brother was frowning, his eyes pinched, but he gave her a small shake of his head. He didn't see a point in stopping this, and it wouldn't change Father's mind.

Marcus got down on his knees at Lucien's feet for the second time that day as he pressed his tunic against the rug, soaking up the wine that had dripped onto the floor. Lucien watched with fire in his eyes.

"I'm afraid I'll have to leave you for a moment," Lucien said as Marcus stood. "I need to change my attire and discipline this careless servant."

Adriana wanted to protest that it had been an accident, to beg Lucien to be merciful, but he'd already said he didn't want her interfering in how he ran his household. What if her protests frustrated him further, and he took it out on Marcus?

Instead, she put on a smile like donning a mask. "Do hurry back, Lucien. Please?"

His returning smile was patronizing. "Of course, my dear bride." He snapped his fingers at his other servant. "Both of you, with me."

Lucien strode out into the corridor, followed closely by Marcus, whose shoulders were hitched up toward his ears, and Lucien's other servant.

After the door shut, she turned to Jairus, her stomach tied in knots. "What will he do? He won't . . . hurt him, will he?"

"Probably." Jairus's frown deepened as his forehead creased. "It's within his legal rights to use corporal punishment on a servant so long as it does not cause the servant's death, maiming, or castration. Strange, though. That Marcus Williams seemed so capable." He shrugged. "Perhaps he was unprepared for such candid mention of the . . . uh . . . second half of the marriage rites. I certainly was."

It had shocked her as well, and she knew why it had upset Marcus. Lucien probably felt humiliated by his *capable* servant making such an error, and from what little she'd observed from him, he was not someone who would take kindly to embarrassment. She clenched her skirt in her sweaty hands, stifling the urge to run after them. She couldn't afford for anyone to realize how much she cared.

CHAPTER 17

The moment they were out in the hall, Thorne grabbed Marcus's undershirt and shoved him forward. "Lead us to your quarters."

Gulping, Marcus bobbed a bow before hurrying down the corridor. He clutched his belt and wine-stained tunic to his chest. Jacob's warning replayed in his mind. What would Thorne do? He struggled to recall what punishments he'd heard of or seen meted out on wayward or careless servants when he'd been a prince. It wasn't something he'd often witnessed, and he'd never cared to punish or tattle on any servants himself. All he knew was that there were a few things forbidden under the law, including killing and breaking of limbs, which was a small comfort. But there were many things a man could suffer without dying or being maimed.

When they reached the room, Thorne and Roger followed him inside. Thorne slammed the door shut, and Edwin and Jacob leapt off their beds with choked "my lord"s.

His mouth dry, Marcus bowed to his liege again. "I'm sorry—"

"You *fool!*" Thorne roared. "You'll pay for your carelessness." The back of his hand smacked across Marcus's face.

The force snapped Marcus's head to the side, and he stumbled sideways, bumping into the edge of someone's bed and tripping. His tunic and belt fell from his hands as he blinked away the dark spots dancing in his eyes.

This was the man Adriana's father wanted her to wed? With a short temper and penchant for violence at such a slight provocation?

It grated against Marcus's sense of pride, but he dropped to his knees and raised his hands in supplication. The last thing he needed was to anger Thorne so much that he was thrown out of the castle. "I was careless, my lord. I beg for your forgiveness."

Thorne's upper lip curled. "You think you can grovel a little and avoid any punishment?"

Marcus blinked. Was being struck not a punishment?

"You spilled my finest wine. Your yearly wages wouldn't purchase another jar that size."

"I'll forfeit two months' wages—"

"That wouldn't even cover the cost of what you wasted." Thorne sneered. "Even if it did, I can't exactly traipse across the sea to Mesti to replace the wine. Nor do I think merely foregoing your wages, when you still have food and shelter, will teach you proper care in your tasks."

A few paces away, Edwin leaned forward, his pale expression strained and eyes wide. Jacob shrank back against the wall, as if afraid of earning a punishment by simply existing in the same room as an irate Thorne. Marcus's heart thudded. What did Thorne have in mind? How worried should he be?

Thorne tapped his chin, his gaze wandering around the room. "How best to remind you, to truly sear into your memory the importance of serving with utmost care for your master's belongings . . . Ah." A wicked smile darkened his face. "*Sear.*" He strode toward the fireplace.

Marcus didn't understand, but Edwin's complexion took on a green tinge, and he looked ready to interfere. Marcus shook his head. No sense in them both getting into trouble. Thorne would mete out his punishment, and it'd be over with.

A dull clang came from near the fireplace as Thorne seized the iron poker and shoved it into the fire.

Sear.

Marcus's mouth went dry, and his stomach twisted. The pain hadn't even happened yet, and he was already trembling. Should he beg again? Or would that only make the punishment worse?

Thorne turned back toward him, the tip of the poker red-hot. He stalked forward with a gleefully savage grin. "Take your shirt off. Unless you want it melted to your skin."

His heart hammering with a more acute fear than when his father had discovered his clandestine meetings with Adriana, Marcus removed his undershirt with shaking hands. Just as the shirt cleared his head and he tossed it aside, something slammed into his chest. Thorne drove him onto his back and pinned him to the floor with a heavy boot.

"Hold still," he taunted.

As the poker moved closer, Marcus clenched his fists, every muscle in his body taut. Fiery heat pressed into his left side. Instinctively he jerked away—or tried to, but he couldn't more than twitch with the weight of Thorne's booted foot holding him down. A scream tore out of his throat, even as Thorne withdrew the poker and lifted his foot.

It had lasted only a brief moment, but pain wracked Marcus's side. His trembling hands edged toward the burning wound, but he forced them down as he writhed, and tears blurred his vision. What could he do? How could he stop the pain? He bit his tongue to silence his whimpers, tasting blood.

Thorne pointed the hot end of the poker at him, and Marcus flinched away. "Let that be a lesson to you." He swung the poker toward Roger, who cowered back, then in Jacob's direction, who curled in on himself. "To all of you. I am a duke and the king's son-in-law, or will be soon, and I will not tolerate disobedience or carelessness." The poker stilled, pointing right at Edwin and sending another jolt of panic through Marcus. "Especially not from hapless peasants I took in out of charity."

He tossed the poker toward the fireplace. The ring of iron striking wood made Marcus flinch again, and the movement sent new stabs of pain through his burn. Thorne strode out of the room, and the door banged shut behind him.

For a moment, no one moved, as if everyone was holding their breath. Then Edwin ran to him, while Roger slunk over to the poker and returned it to its spot by the fireplace.

"Marcus . . ." Edwin's throat bobbed as his hands hovered over the wound like he also didn't know what to do. "I'm sorry—I'm so sorry; I should have protect—"

"Oh, shut up." Marcus clenched his teeth. "I'm in too much pain to argue with you right now."

Jacob eased away from where he'd been cowering against the wall. "You should visit the castle healer as soon as possible."

Edwin nodded. "That's right. They told us on the tour where to find him. We might have to wait if he's tending to a noble, but he's sworn to help anyone who asks." He handed Marcus his undershirt. "Come on. I'll get you a different tunic."

Marcus finished pulling off his undershirt and winced at the sight of his side. The shiny deep-red wound was as long as his forefinger, nearly two finger-widths across, and covered in swelling blisters. Burning pain radiated out from it and was on the brink of driving him mad.

The healer, a man named Alban with long gray hair pinned up in a topknot, stared before handing him a dripping cloth. "Hold this against the burn." He met Marcus's eyes. "From a hot poker, you say? And this happened how?"

Marcus didn't feel inclined to lie for the benefit of Thorne's reputation. "A punishment administered by my lord for spilled wine." He relaxed against the back of the wood chair as he pressed the cloth over the wound, the cool water immediately easing some of the white-hot pain.

Alban's lips thinned beneath his gray beard, his eyes flashing disapproval, but he said nothing as he turned away and started grabbing things from a cabinet and off a table. What was there to say? Legally, Thorne had done nothing wrong.

"At least it's red and shiny. And it hurts?" Alban glanced over his shoulder as Marcus nodded. "Good. If it didn't, that would mean it's much worse. I wish we could have gotten water on that sooner, though." He shook his head as he continued mixing and grinding ingredients in a small mortar.

"What's that?" Edwin asked.

"Burn salve. With a little magic."

Marcus leaned sideways to peer around the healer's back. "You're an enchanter?"

"One with minimal skills, but enough that I can speed up

healing for most things and strengthen the beneficial properties of plants and foods." Alban stilled, and a faint green glow briefly shone from the mortar. "That should do it." He flipped over a sand timer about as large as Marcus's fist and turned to face him, flexing and shaking the fingers of his right hand. "Does your lord require you back soon?"

"I don't think so." He hoped not. Likely Thorne wouldn't want to see him again for a while and would be busy with Adriana. The thought turned his stomach. It didn't matter whether he got out unscathed—whatever it took, even if it killed him, he would not let Adriana marry that villain.

"Good. You'll want to keep the cloth on until that timer runs out. If the cloth stops feeling cool, we'll rewet it. After that we'll dry the burn, apply the salve, and cover it. You should come by tomorrow so I can clean it and decide if it needs more salve or just to be covered to prevent infection until it heals."

Marcus nodded. That sounded manageable. "Is your hand all right?"

"Hm? Oh." The healer continued flexing his fingers. "Yes. Using my magic can make my extremities numb. Have to wake them back up. I'll be fine momentarily."

After a moment, Alban turned to tidy up his supplies. "Have you been with Lord Thorne long?" His carefully neutral tone and the way he avoided looking directly at Marcus suggested the innocent question was more than it appeared.

"No. Only two days."

"I was going to ask if he's usually so vindictive, but if he jumped to this so quickly, I suppose that answers my question." Alban slumped back against the edge of the table, his expression worried.

Was the healer also concerned about how Thorne would treat Adriana? "I'm only a servant," Marcus said, feeling like he should offer some reassurance. "I'm sure he won't treat the princess like this." He'd make sure Thorne wouldn't have the chance if it was the last thing he did.

Alban's countenance grew sadder. "It's my granddaughter. She's the princess's maid. She's supposed to go with the princess to join Thorne's household . . ." The older man abruptly spun around, but Marcus saw him wipe at his eyes.

There was nothing Marcus could say. He could offer to protect Leena, but he couldn't even protect himself, so Alban wouldn't be reassured. If only he could tell the old healer that the wedding wouldn't happen. There was no way he could explain without putting himself and any chance of stopping the wedding in jeopardy.

Perhaps he was delusional for thinking that a hunted former prince turned servant had a chance of disrupting the plans of kings and lords. But he had failed to protect his subjects from suffering the ravages of war.

He would not fail to protect the woman he loved.

CHAPTER 18

The remainder of the day dragged on, every minute longer than the last. Adriana couldn't feel relaxed around Lucien, not after glimpsing the controlled fury that she feared he had unleashed on Marcus in private. She'd dared to ask how he'd punished the servant, but Lucien had only told her that such tasks fell under his purview and that she needn't worry about it and could be assured Marcus wouldn't make such a mistake again. Lords were allowed to do a great many terrible things to punish a servant, and the fear that somewhere in the castle Marcus was bleeding or beaten black and blue plagued her.

It was worse when Father called Jairus away, leaving her alone with Lucien and two silent servants, one of the castle's and one of Lucien's. Somehow, though, she made it through. She even got revenge for his boring prattling about himself when she pulled out some embroidery and told him all about the various stitches and minutiae of embroidering while he clearly didn't care.

They ate supper in the great hall, and Adriana retired

immediately afterward, complaining of a headache. She couldn't stand to spend another moment in Lucien's company.

The evening couldn't end fast enough. Leena coaxed her into taking a bath to unwind and pass some time, but after her hair was combed through and scrunched and twisted and patted dry into springy curls, it still was too early for her to sneak downstairs. She tried to read but couldn't focus.

At long last, it was time. Adriana lit a candle and hurried through the castle in her slippers, listening carefully to avoid any of the few guardsmen that patrolled the halls. When she reached the study, she pushed the door open and blinked against the light from the fire. A tall figure wearing a tunic that fell to his boots stood silhouetted before the fireplace, and the sudden fear possessed her that it might be her brother or father rather than Marcus.

"Adriana," Marcus said, his tone warm and soothing.

Her heart leapt as she hurried inside, easing the door closed behind her before rushing to him. He stood straight and tall, his arms hanging loosely at his sides, and not a single bruise marked his smiling face. Relief coursed through her. She set the candle on the fireplace mantel and threw her arms around his waist.

A muffled cry escaped Marcus as he flinched. She quickly released him. His right hand reached toward his left ribs, and his fingertips brushed the fabric of his tunic before he dropped his hand back to his side. His pained expression smoothed into a tight smile. Her joy evaporated.

"Did Lucien hurt you?"

Marcus gulped and glanced away.

Taking his hand, Adriana led him over to sit beside her on the chaise. She interlaced their fingers as she peered up at him. "Marcus—"

"You can't marry him, no matter what." The words held a frantic, pleading edge. "I don't care what it takes or what I have to do to stop this wedding—"

"Did he harm you? Just for spilling wine?"

Firelight flickered in the whites of his wide eyes. His shoulders scrunched toward his neck, but he winced and relaxed his posture.

"Marcus, please. What happened?"

He took a deep breath and angled his face away from her. "Lord Thorne believed I needed a reminder not to be careless with my master's things. A lesson seared into my side with a hot fire-poker."

Nausea churned Adriana's stomach while rage burned through her veins. "How bad is it?"

"I'm fine."

"Don't lie to me," she said gently.

Marcus grimaced. "It hurt like torment and looks terrible, but your healer said it's good it hurts. If it didn't, that would mean the damage was more severe. It still burns a little and hurts when bumped, but not nearly as bad as it would without your healer's magic-infused salves." He finally looked at her, his eyebrows knitting together. "I searched Lord Thorne's room, but I didn't find anything incriminating. Have you come up with anything to prevent the marriage?"

"Is this not enough?" She thrust her hand toward his side. "We have proof of his cruelty!"

Marcus lifted his free hand to cradle her cheek. "I have a treatable burn that at worst will scar. It won't impair me. He is within his legal rights as my master."

"Don't call him that," she said fervently.

He gave a sad chuckle. "It tastes rotten on my tongue."

Adriana rested her palm against his neck and leaned closer to him. "He's awful. But you're right. Nothing he has done will change my father's mind."

Marcus suddenly went rigid and very still.

"What's wrong?"

"What if . . ." His fingers tightened around hers. "He hasn't done anything illegal *yet*. What if he does? What would change your father's mind? Would a broken leg?"

With a gasp, she leaned back, her hand moving to clench his tunic. "Absolutely not. Whether you're thinking of goading him or harming yourself, neither is acceptable to me; do you understand?"

His palm slipped off her cheek as he slumped. "All right. But we have to do something."

"We have tomorrow and half of the next day to find a solution." That was cutting it far too close, but she didn't want Marcus to do something stupid out of desperation. "We will find a way."

He nodded. "I know. I won't let him hurt you." His voice pitched lower, a fierce protectiveness burning through his words as his face set into chiseled determination.

An involuntary whimper caught in the back of Adriana's throat. Oh, the things that man did to her heart.

Releasing her grip on his tunic, she scooted over to the low back at the far end of the chaise and gently pulled him down until he was lying with his head resting on her lap. There. That should be less overwhelming than sitting there staring into his brown eyes.

"I love you," she whispered, running her fingers through the long strands of his black hair.

Only the heat of the fire and the weight of his head on her lap convinced her this moment wasn't a dream conjured by her heartbroken imagination.

Marcus stared up at her, the adoration in his eyes making him more irresistible. "I love you."

If only she were marrying Marcus in a day and a half . . . wait.

"What if we got married first?"

He frowned. "What?"

She sat straighter, her fingers stilling in his hair as the obvious solution presented itself. "All we have to do is get married and consummate the marriage. Then I'm married and can't be married to Lucien Thorne."

Marcus didn't appear to share her excitement as his mouth pinched. "There's an easy way around that. Make you a widow."

Her throat caught. "But—"

"Especially if we ran away. Your father and Lucien could cover it up, or if word got out, claim that I had kidnapped you because I hate your father for killing my family. Your father wants Thorne's money, and he's already demonstrated he'll gladly get rid of me. Based on Thorne's pride and a comment he made today about being a duke soon, I'm confident he wants the title and prestige he'll get as your husband. I doubt he'll care if we've . . ." Marcus reddened and coughed. "You know."

She couldn't help a little smirk. "Don't you want to . . . you know?" She waggled her eyebrows.

Somehow, he turned redder as he bolted upright. "Are you . . . do you . . . I do, but not . . . You know I want to marry you, but we . . . not . . ."

Adriana laughed and came to his rescue. "Not while we're

meeting in secret to steal moments together and when we don't know what the future holds? Agreed." She tilted her head down, giving what she hoped was a sultry look. "But I hope we can get married soon."

"Me too." Marcus tugged on his collar, then stood. "But for now, we should both rest. Meet here again tomorrow at the same time? Assuming we haven't managed to get rid of Thorne before then?"

She nodded and stood as well. "Be careful tomorrow, all right?"

"I will."

She went up on her toes and kissed him. Their kiss was brief but sweet, and she drew away even though she wanted to linger. She would let that brief kiss be a promise between them, and the thought of more be a motivation to find Lucien Thorne's downfall.

CHAPTER 19

One of the Faines' servants knocked on their door early the next morning and announced that Lord Thorne had summoned the Williams brothers to his chamber. Marcus shared a worried look with Edwin before they threw on their own clothing and hurried to Lord Thorne's room.

"You don't suppose he's still angry enough to punish us both, do you?" Marcus asked as they bounded up a spiral staircase in one of the towers.

"I hope not." But Edwin didn't look very sure of that.

Marcus hadn't even finished knocking when Thorne called them inside. The nobleman was sitting on the edge of his bed as he put on his boots. The top section of his hair was done in intricate braids with the silver hair stick tucked into the leather tie. How early did the man get up to have his hair looking so neat already?

Thorne finished lacing his boot and looked up, his gaze sweeping up and down them both as the corners of his mouth turned down further. "What are you wearing?"

Marcus glanced at his tunic. The ankle-length tunic was made of soft wool in a rich crimson and split down the front and back to allow ease of movement. Black and silver embroidery in a repeating pattern of arches and points finished all of the hems—the collar, the cuffs, and the bottom hem, including the slits. It was hardly the fanciest tunic he'd ever worn, but it was nice and too long for a servant doing manual labor.

"One of my tunics, my lord?"

"Who was your last lord, anyway?" Thorne crossed his arms, still scrutinizing them.

Marcus hesitated, wondering how best to answer that. Perhaps the near truth would be safest. "Prince Arlius Alimer, my lord."

Thorne's eyebrows reached for his hairline. "You . . ." He tossed his head back and laughed. "No, that makes sense, actually." His eyes narrowed. "Other than the part where you're not dead."

Right, Thorne supposedly valued loyalty. He'd be suspicious of deserters.

Marcus inclined his head. "When King Mortimer's siege began, we were away on an errand for Prince Arlius. We couldn't get back into the castle and hadn't been sent out with any weapons, so there was no way for us to aid our liege. We lay low and waited for the battle to be over."

Thorne eyed them. "Weapons? Are you saying you know

how to use them?"

Drat it. He'd forgotten he didn't want to reveal that information.

Edwin shrugged. "Passably, my lord. We often attended the elder two princes, who liked to know those serving them could be relied on in more ways than one."

"I see." Thorne made a humming noise in the back of his throat. "Well, I suppose this will do, even if yours is ostentatious, Marcus. At least Edwin's looks like a servant's tunic."

Of course Edwin's tunic, with its sparse black embroidery on dusty green fabric that came down to his knees, looked more like a servant's, since it actually was. Marcus wished he'd paid more heed to what he was putting on.

"Are we to attend you today, my lord?" Edwin asked.

"I'm granting you both a chance to redeem yourselves from Marcus's error yesterday." Thorne's expression turned hard and foreboding. "If either of you fails or embarrasses me today, I will not be merciful to both of you."

They bowed in tandem, both murmuring, "Yes, my lord."

Marcus shoved down his panic. He would need to be focused and completely ignore Adriana and anything Thorne might say about their marriage. If he got distracted and did something wrong again, Edwin would suffer, too. Edwin had already done more than enough suffering on his behalf.

"I'm unsure what we'll be doing today," Thorne said, "but

whatever it is, your assignment is the same—anticipate my needs, obey quickly and deferentially, and in general ensure your behavior reflects well on me. Understood?"

As they murmured their assent, Thorne stood and stepped forward, but he must not have realized how close he was sitting to the corner of the bed and the low arc of the tied-back curtains draping from the corner post. The curved end of his silver hair stick caught on the thick fabric, momentarily tugging him backward before the stick slipped free and was left dangling from the curtain as Thorne's eyes went round as saucers.

Had that been all, Marcus would have been fighting the urge to laugh.

Instead, the blood drained from his face as he stared, his heartbeat spiking.

With a snarled curse, Thorne spun away from them, hunching as he snatched up the hair stick and stabbed it into his hair. But it was too late to hide what Marcus had seen.

Green, snakelike scales covered the entire right half of Thorne's face and his clawed right hand. One normal and one slitted reptilian eye blinked at them, the latter a mottled yellow and black. The right half of his mouth had no lips, partially showing his teeth and twisting awkwardly where the scaley skin melded with human flesh. The hair growing out of the scaled half of his head was thin and dull with a greenish sheen.

The hair stick back in place, Thorne whipped around to

face them, his appearance returned to normal. In two quick strides, he was in front of them, his hands closing around their throats as he slammed them back into the stone wall.

"You saw *nothing*." His grip on Marcus's throat tightened to the point of strangulation as he pushed Marcus and Edwin up the wall until they were standing on the balls of their feet. "You saw nothing, and neither of you will say a word otherwise to me or another living soul, or I will kill you both. Slowly and painfully." He squeezed harder, and Marcus grabbed at Thorne's hand, trying to pull it away from his throat to no effect as his vision clouded over.

At last Thorne released them, and they both collapsed to the ground, coughing and sputtering between gasping air into their bursting lungs.

A hand roughly grasped Marcus's hair and yanked, forcing him to look up at Thorne.

"The only reason I'm not killing you right this moment is because it'd be messy and difficult to hide. But I can find a way to make you disappear that won't draw attention if you cause trouble. But you're not going to tell a soul, are you, Marcus Williams?"

"No, my lord." His voice rasped.

Thorne knocked Marcus aside and then grasped Edwin by his hair. "And you, Edwin? Did you see anything unusual?"

Edwin shuddered. "No, my lord."

Thorne shoved him so hard he sprawled onto his side. As Thorne straightened, he brushed his hands over his tunic and adjusted his belt before smoothing his palm over his braids.

Gingerly rubbing his aching throat, Marcus looked over at Edwin, reassuring himself that his friend was all right. As he sat up, Edwin ran his fingertips over the red marks on his throat, and his light-copper braids were in complete disarray, but he otherwise appeared uninjured.

"Get up," Thorne said as he glared down his nose at them.

His legs were a touch shaky, but Marcus got to his feet, and so did Edwin.

"Your hair's a mess. Tidy yourselves up and then eat your breakfast quickly. I expect you both to meet me in the great hall to wait on me during breakfast. Go!"

They nearly tripped over themselves in their haste to leave the room.

What *was* Thorne? A human cursed by some vengeful witch? Or, as his unnerving strength suggested, not human at all?

Roger sneered, asking what they'd done in only a few minutes to get themselves into trouble. Jacob appeared sympathetic, while the other servants eyed their bruising necks with trepidation.

They fixed their hair as quickly as possible. Neither of them spoke. Marcus didn't know what to say. What horrible situation had he gotten them into? At least he had an answer to saving Adriana. Surely King Mortimer would never give his daughter to that . . . thing.

The problem would be telling them. If he tried to address any of the royal family in front of Thorne, it'd be obvious what he was doing, and Thorne would stop him. He could try to remove Thorne's hair stick, but Thorne would never let him get close enough. Either option might end with Thorne making good on his threat and killing him before he had a chance to warn Adriana.

The wedding wasn't until tomorrow, and he planned to meet with Adriana that night. He just needed to get through today without any further incidents and warn her. During the wedding ceremony, she'd be able to reach the hair stick before they took their vows. That should put an end to all of this.

Unless . . . would Thorne harm her if she did that? He was incredibly strong, and if he wasn't human, who knew what other secrets or perhaps magical powers he was hiding?

If only he could talk to Adriana alone now. He wouldn't form a plan without her input. It was her future at stake more than his. Edwin was involved in this, too. He'd have to take Edwin with him to his meeting with Adriana. Between the three of them, surely they could strategize a way to expose Thorne to the king without risking harm to either Edwin or Adriana.

That was a problem for later. The current problem was getting through the day without invoking Thorne's wrath.

After a rushed breakfast of oatmeal, Marcus turned to Edwin as they walked down a hall.

"Don't," Edwin said before Marcus could speak. "It's not your fault. No one could have seen *that* coming." He glanced over. "How's your side?"

Marcus winced. "Tender, but that healer's salve did wonders. Wish he could put it on my throat."

Edwin touched his own neck with a grimace. "Agreed."

"Tonight," Marcus whispered, leaning closer, "come with me. We'll make a plan."

To his relief, Edwin nodded rather than arguing. "Whatever he is, he needs to be exposed. But we need to be even more careful, or we might only make things worse."

"Agreed." He opened his mouth to apologize for his recent carelessness that had placed them in this position, but he stopped. Edwin was right.

Marcus hadn't caused Thorne to be wicked, much like he hadn't caused his father to be power hungry and start a war. He'd been foolish to rush into serving Lord Thorne, but that didn't mean he deserved to suffer for his mistake. Thorne could just as easily have turned out to be a good man.

But he did have a responsibility to act when he had the ability to do so to prevent evil, and he had the capability of learning from his mistakes. He'd be more cautious, especially where the wellbeing of those he cared about was involved, and he wouldn't stand idly by, hoping and wishing for change while not risking himself.

CHAPTER 20

Stifling a yawn, Adriana entered the great hall to find her father and brother and Lucien already there. Besides staying up to see Marcus, she'd struggled to go to sleep afterward, her mind wide awake thinking of him and how to get rid of Lucien.

Unfortunately, no brilliant ideas had come to her, other than an incomplete plan to slip Lucien a sleeping draught so he wouldn't attend the wedding. All she really had to show for her lack of sleep were shadows under her eyes.

As Adriana crossed to the table at the head of the room, her gaze fell on Marcus and Edwin standing unobtrusively in the corner. She'd almost overlooked them, and she had to stifle an involuntary smile at seeing Marcus. What would it be like to see him every day and not have to hide her joy? She wanted more than anything to find out, and that meant she needed a reason why Lucien was an unacceptable son-in-law . . .

Her attention caught on Marcus's throat, and she stumbled and tensed.

Red bruises encircled Marcus's neck—actually, both his and Edwin's throats bore clustered bruises that looked suspiciously like . . .

Her gaze swung to Lucien. "Did you strangle them?" The words spilled out as she motioned toward Marcus and Edwin. Perhaps showing she cared was a bad idea, but fury muddled her thoughts—besides, even if it hadn't been Marcus and Edwin, she wouldn't stand for someone strangling their servants.

Lucien glanced at the men. "Does it matter what happened? Their discipline is my business."

"Father—"

"Sit down, Adriana." Father's mouth pinched with displeasure. "They're standing, aren't they? They're fine. As Lucien said, so long as he doesn't kill or maim them, how he disciplines his servants is his own business and his legal right."

"Then change the law! You're the king, use it!"

Had she just said that out loud? In front of all the knights and attendants and servants in the great hall? She wished she could sink through the floor, especially as Father glared at her with the heat of ten suns, but she forced her spine straight.

"I don't wish to marry a man who treats his servants so harshly."

Lucien inclined his head. "Perhaps you can tell me what punishments you find both tolerable and effective and I can implement those to better please you."

Father waved a hand. "There, you see? He's perfectly reasonable. Come sit down."

Jairus gave her a pleading look and discreetly flicked his hand in the direction of her chair. The eyes of the entire hall bored into her. Could she leverage the audience against Father? She looked back to Marcus. He gave a subtle shake of his head, and his expression seemed to caution her to wait. Perhaps he had learned something—was that why Lucien had hurt them? If whatever they knew had made Lucien that angry, it had to be significant. But if Marcus wasn't saying anything, there must also be a reason for his deferral.

Reluctantly, Adriana took her seat at Lucien's side.

A few times during breakfast she snuck sideways glances at Marcus and Edwin to reassure herself they were still there and all right. Once Marcus caught her looking and sent her a small, quick smile. It brought a tentative smile to her own lips.

After breakfast, they retired to the sitting room, and Jairus challenged Lucien to a game of chess, which turned into a rematch, which turned into best two out of three . . . It was rather boring, but considering the alternative was talking to Lucien, Adriana didn't mind. Besides, this way, she could continue sneaking glances at the man she actually cared about.

This time they returned to the great hall for dinner, which she appreciated. It was less awkward, and it meant Lucien couldn't ask Marcus or Edwin to serve him. She was not in the mood to watch him order either of them around.

Both young men left with Lucien's permission to get their own food, and Adriana watched them go. Lucien pulled out her chair for her and then pushed her up to the table. He leaned down over her shoulder, on the side further from Father.

"Does my servant capture your fancy?" he whispered close by her ear. "You seem awfully interested in him and more eager to look at him than me."

Her face heated. "No. I'm merely concerned for his health and welfare. Both of them. Both of their health."

"And he hasn't . . . sought you out in private? Either of them?"

A small jolt went through Adriana, and she knew she had to be blushing now. "Of course not," she hissed, hoping her panic came across as anger. "Do you think I'd allow some male servant to see me in private? How dare you slander me like that."

"It's not you I'm worried about." Lucien patted her shoulder before taking his seat to her right.

What did that mean? Did Lucien know that Marcus had snuck out last night and suspect where he'd gone? Was that why he'd choked Marcus and Edwin?

Although Marcus hadn't looked worried. Unless his smiles were lies meant to put her at ease? She'd drive herself mad with such ruminations.

They were nearly done eating when Marcus and Edwin

returned to the same corner they had occupied at breakfast. Lucien eyed them as they walked past and glanced between her and Marcus, his expression unreadable, so she fixated on her remaining food, determined to appear uninterested in Marcus's arrival.

After dinner, Lucien suggested they go for a ride. That would have been perfectly agreeable, as the sun was bright and warm, glistening on the fresh snow that had fallen overnight, and riding required that there be space between their respective steeds. Unfortunately, Lucien commanded Marcus and Edwin to accompany them and carry blankets and canteens of water in case they had need of them, and then Father advised them to also bring some sacks of candied nuts. While she rode with Lucien and Jairus, Marcus and Edwin jogged after them on foot with packs strapped on their backs.

Normally Adriana loved riding, but she didn't love it when Lucien kept urging his horse into a canter and Marcus and Edwin had to run to catch up, sweat beading on their faces despite the chill. What if they caught cold? If their wet clothing and the cold air dropped their temperature enough, they could be in danger. But if she asked Lucien to return to the castle, would that make him more suspicious of Marcus?

She glanced back at Marcus and Edwin as they struggled through a windblown snowbank that came halfway up their calves. Their chests heaved with every breath that fogged the air in front of their red faces.

"Lucien, you'll run your servants into the ground or risk losing their toes to frostbite." Adriana turned her horse toward the castle. "We need to return. Besides, my ears are getting cold."

"Marcus," Lucien called as he wheeled his own horse around. "Bring some of those candied nuts for me. And give Princess Adriana a blanket to cover her head and warm her ears."

"We don't need to delay for that—"

"They'll be fine. Right, boys?"

Panting, Marcus jogged over to Lucien's horse. "Yes, my lord."

Jairus reined in his horse beside Adriana's and frowned. "You do seem to have little regard for your servants' health."

"A servant's health is secondary to his lord's needs," Lucien said with a shrug. He took the small pouch of candied nuts from Marcus.

His eyes lowered, Marcus shuffled over to Adriana's horse and held a blanket up to her. She wanted to ask if he was truly all right but didn't dare with Lucien watching them.

"A servant in poor health can't properly see to their lord's needs," Jairus countered. "And servants are men and women who offer us service in exchange for their pay and care. A lord's duty is to his people, including his servants. Why should a serv-ant continue to work for someone who abuses them when an-other lord will protect his subjects as he ought?"

Adriana smiled at her brother as she took the blanket from Marcus. Their gloved fingers brushed against each other. "Exactly. Servants are just as human as their lords."

"But hardly deserving of equal respect." Lucien sniffed. "Respect is earned."

"Perhaps, but human dignity shouldn't be earned." She turned an icy glare on her betrothed. "And what, in your estimation, deserves respect? Am I deserving of your respect?"

Out of the corner of her eye, she caught Marcus's approving smirk.

"Of course, Adriana." Lucien prodded his horse forward. "But perhaps we should discuss this inside. After all, you wanted to return, yet you're the one stalling while my servants stand in the cold."

"We could let them ride with us," Jairus said. "Then we'd return faster, and they'd be less likely to freeze."

Adriana could have hugged him, but Lucien laughed.

"An amusing jest, Your Highness. As if we'd share our mounts with snow-dampened servants."

"Then they can ride with Jairus and me," she exclaimed, indignation crawling over her skin. How in Miraveld could Father be all right with marrying her to this churl? "Climb on behind me, Marcus."

Lucien and Marcus both gaped at her. Belatedly, her mind caught up to her, but it was too late.

"That would be far outside of the bounds of propriety," Lucien protested.

"Adriana and I could share a horse and the servants could share the other," Jairus said. "That would hardly be improper."

"No!" Adriana opened and closed her mouth, searching for a reason why that wouldn't work.

"Neither of us knows how to ride," Marcus said with a small bow. "I'm unsure it would be wise for my brother or myself to attempt it for the first time in the snow."

Jairus made a humming noise. "And my steed is spirited. Misbehaves if there isn't a steady hand on the reins."

"I'm not letting an inexperienced rider handle my horse, either," Adriana declared. She waved to Marcus. "Hurry and get on behind me, then. I'm to be your lady, which means you're to serve me, so you may as well start obeying me now."

Marcus's mouth twisted as if he was trying not to laugh, and there was something dangerously flirtatious in his eyes that made her very grateful his back was to Lucien.

"Come on, then—Edward, was it?" Jairus asked.

"Edwin, my lord," he said as he edged closer.

"Marcus and Edwin," Jairus mused. "Those names sound so familiar . . ." Panic leapt up Adriana's throat, but he was already shaking his head. "Well, up you come, Edwin."

Similar fear shone in Marcus's expression for a moment, but he blinked and it was gone. As Edwin approached Jairus's horse, Marcus reached up and grabbed the cantle of Adriana's saddle, his fingers tucking between the top edge of the cantle and the base of her spine, and then he swung up behind her with a muscular agility that caused her breath to catch.

Before Lucien could argue, Adriana urged her horse into a trot and then a canter. With every beat of her horse's hooves, Marcus's knuckles brushed against her lower back. The wind whipped around her ears, and she realized that despite her hair being tucked into her cloak, with her hood down, Marcus was probably getting a face-full of curls. That was less romantic than she'd pictured sharing a horse to be.

"Thorne has a secret," Marcus said quietly, close by the back of her head. "If we can expose him, there won't be a wedding. That's all I dare say right now. I don't want to act too soon and risk anyone getting hurt."

How would exposing this secret result in someone getting hurt? Remembering the bruises on Marcus's and Edwin's throats, she decided not to push it. She would trust Marcus and wait until tonight.

When they arrived at the stables, a servant was waiting for them.

"Your Highness," the man said, bowing to Jairus. "Your father the king requests your presence in his study at once. He has been waiting for some time."

Jairus winced. "Apologies, Lord Lucien, Adriana. It seems

I have to leave you, at least for a while." He leapt off his horse and rushed toward the castle.

Adriana bit her tongue to stifle an objection. Losing Jairus as her support and buffer after challenging Lucien was poor timing. Marcus jumped down and held out his hand to help her dismount, but as she reached for him, Lucien shoved him out of the way so hard he slammed into the side of an empty stall with a groan.

"Marcus!"

Her horse skittered as it pinned its ears back, and she had to turn her attention to calming the animal. Lucien seized the reins and held out his other hand to her as the horse calmed.

With a gulp, she took his hand and dismounted. His fingers tightened around hers, and he leaned over her, making her feel small and trapped between his hulking figure and the horse at her back.

"Tell me again, Adriana," Lucien said in a low voice. "Does my servant capture your fancy?"

"I'm not dignifying that with an answer." She tried to pull her hand free, but he only held on tighter.

Behind him, Edwin checked on Marcus, who winced before straightening.

"Is everything all right, Your Highness?" A stable hand edged closer, a pitchfork casually grasped in one hand.

Lucien stepped back, no longer looming over her. While it

would be risky for a servant to attack a lord, if the servant was defending his own lady, the servant likely wouldn't be blamed. Not to mention an altercation because the groom was acting threatening toward the bride-to-be might ruin the wedding. Thinking about it that way, Adriana almost wished the servant hadn't intervened so soon and that Lucien had done something worse than squeeze her hand.

"Apologies." Lucien sounded anything but apologetic. He offered her his arm. "Shall we return to the castle?"

Ignoring his arm and marching past him was sorely tempting, but that might attract more suspicion. She tucked her hand into the crook of his elbow and let him lead her around the castle and back inside. Edwin and Marcus trailed after them, keeping a respectful distance.

Once inside, Lucien claimed he needed to use the water closet and promised to meet her shortly in the sitting room. Marcus and Edwin trailed after him, and her stomach churned. Would he hurt Marcus because of what she'd done?

When Lucien arrived at the sitting room, it was with Edwin and a female servant in tow. Edwin followed his lord in with his head bowed, and he didn't acknowledge Adriana. He didn't move as if he had been injured, and she didn't see any new bruises, but where was Marcus?

She didn't dare reveal her fear by asking what Lucien had done with him. Instead, she plastered on a smile and asked if

Lucien had done much traveling. That got him started on the places he'd been and what he liked or hated about them, so she didn't have to talk often—until he finally turned the question back on her, and, unfortunately, she hadn't traveled much. Thankfully, Father and Jairus arrived then, and the three of them turned to discussing challenges with transitioning Aedyllan back into a singular monarchy after almost a century as a conglomerate of equal principalities.

Ensuring Lucien wasn't watching her, Adriana caught Edwin's gaze and mouthed, "Marcus?"

Edwin winced, but mouthed back, "Fine."

The hours crawled by until at last it was time to sneak downstairs to meet with Marcus.

CHAPTER 21

Marcus and Edwin crept through the castle until they reached the sitting room at last. A bit of light showed beneath the door, indicating someone must already be inside. Marcus hoped it was Adriana. If anyone else was in that sitting room, it would be nearly impossible to justify their presence.

He opened the door to find Adriana pacing in front of the fireplace. Her relieved expression quickly fled, replaced by distress.

"Oh, Marcus . . ."

He'd gotten a glimpse of himself in the small mirror on a wall in the servants' room, so he knew it wasn't a good look. His right eye was red and blue and almost swollen shut, and purplish bruises mottled his jawline and left cheekbone. At least she couldn't see the bruises on his ribs. Nothing that wouldn't heal, but his entire head ached—although pain had been only part of the goal.

Thorne had interrogated him about whether he somehow had an illicit relationship with Adriana, which Marcus and

Edwin had staunchly denied, but Thorne had noticed too much between them—too many stolen glances on both of their parts. He was convinced that although they hadn't done anything yet, they were planning on it after the wedding. Thorne had vowed that he wouldn't let Marcus near Adriana, but he also had wanted to "mess up that face of yours she likes so much."

Adriana hurried over to him, her lower lip trembling.

"I'm all right—"

The door behind them opened again. Marcus and Edwin spun around, Edwin placing himself between the intruder and Marcus. He braced himself, expecting to see that somehow, despite how careful they'd been, Thorne had caught them, but instead . . .

"Jairus?" Adriana gasped.

The crown prince closed the door and leaned back against it, his arms crossed. "You're looking spry for a dead man, Prince Marcus Alimer."

Something seemed to lodge in Marcus's throat.

"It was bothering me," Jairus said. "Marcus isn't an uncommon name, so I'd dismissed it as unfortunate timing. Neither is Edwin, but the combination tickled my memories. Then with how Adriana was acting toward you . . . and the look you gave her before mounting her horse . . ." He wrinkled his nose. "I finally put it together and remembered that

Adriana had mentioned Prince Marcus's servant, Edwin. I wasn't completely certain I was correct, though, so I kept an eye on the hall outside of Adriana's room and followed her down here, then waited in the dark corridor."

Marcus sighed, his shoulders drooping. To have gotten this close . . . At least Jairus wasn't armed. Marcus could still warn them about Thorne before he was executed.

Adriana stepped around Marcus. "Jairus, please—"

"I'm not telling Father." Jairus straightened and uncrossed his arms. "I'm assuming you're all here to plan how to stop the wedding. I'm here to help."

Had he heard correctly? Marcus blinked. Edwin's stance eased, and he glanced back at Marcus as if asking *do we believe him?*

"You . . . will help us?" Marcus asked.

Jairus's eyebrows drew together. "Of course. She's my baby sister. I want her to be happy, and I don't want her to be with a man I doubt will treat her well." He shook his head, his blond hair spilling over his shoulders. "But Father refuses to listen to me. I hope you have a plan."

"Not exactly," Marcus said, "but I have information."

Jairus motioned toward the chairs around the fireplace, and they all sat down, Marcus and Adriana sitting beside each other on the chaise. She took his left hand, clasping it between both of hers in her lap.

"Lucien Thorne is . . . well, actually I don't know what he is," Marcus said. Why did every word have to make his face hurt so much? "Have you noticed he is always wearing that silver hair stick?"

Jairus nodded. "I found it slightly odd but assumed he was ostentatious. Why?"

"It's enchanted," Edwin interjected. "This morning it accidentally came out of his hair, and his appearance changed. He's . . . it's like he's half snake or lizard or something."

"What?" Adriana's hands tightened around Marcus's. Jairus looked skeptical.

"When the silver piece is in his hair, he looks normal," Edwin continued. Marcus was grateful, as it meant he could keep his own face still. "If the stick is removed, the right half of his body is covered in green scales. His right hand has claws, and his eye is yellow and serpent-like. Either he's cursed or he's not human."

Adriana shivered.

"Either way, Father won't let Adriana marry something so hideous." Jairus slumped back, his relief evident. "We just have to make him remove the hair stick. Why didn't you tell us earlier?"

Marcus shook his head. "We only discovered it this morning. I couldn't risk Thorne realizing what I was doing and stopping me before I had the chance to explain." He motioned to his face, then his throat. "These bruises might have been because he was jealous for Adriana's attention, but these and the matching ones on Edwin's neck were because he said he'd kill us both if we told anyone. We're not even certain if he's human, and if he's not, what magical powers he might have. I didn't want to rush to expose him and cause either Edwin or Adriana to be harmed."

Jairus's mouth pinched. "Wise. I'll gather the knights and we'll confront him—"

"No."

Marcus turned to look at Adriana so quickly his neck popped. "What?"

"I . . . I have an idea." She locked eyes with Marcus. "It's dangerous because it might not work. Even if it does, it may still be dangerous. But if it works . . . it would solve everything. Not just stopping the wedding, but saving you, too."

"Only if it will save you." Marcus brushed some of her springy curls behind her ear. "I can wait." Or sacrifice himself entirely, if need be, but she wouldn't want to hear that.

Adriana took a deep breath, then explained her plan.

After much discussion, they had a plan, with several backup plans in place at Jairus's insistence. Most of the risks fell on Marcus, but he preferred that. He'd do whatever was necessary to ensure that Lucien never laid a finger on Adriana.

Before they returned to their rooms, Jairus escorted Marcus and Edwin to see the healer for their bruises. Lucien had left Marcus locked in Lucien's chamber until after supper, so by the time Marcus had gone to the healer's room, it was empty. Jairus insisted Alban was fine with being awakened. Besides, they needed Alban's help for part of their plan.

Partway there, Jairus stopped in a cold hallway and turned to Marcus, his gaze steady in the light of the candle he held. "If this plan succeeds, are you sure you want to swear fealty to the man who killed your entire family and tried to kill you? Just to be able to marry Adriana?"

"There's no *just* about marrying her," Marcus said, keeping most of his irritation out of his tone. "But yes. My father brought his destruction on his own head. If he hadn't been greedy, stirred up revolt in Nydellan Principality, and orchestrated a cowardly attack on Faine Principality while its prince was gone, Alimer Castle would likely still stand. Furthermore, I desire to avoid any more conflicts. If bending the knee to your father is what it takes to secure Aedyllan's peace, I'll gladly do it."

Jairus nodded with a slight smile and then continued leading the way to Alban's bedchamber.

While the healer tended Marcus's wounds, Jairus and Edwin explained what they planned to do. As Marcus had guessed, Alban was more than happy to provide what they needed.

When Marcus awoke the next morning, his bruises had mostly faded to green and yellow, and he could open his right eye almost all the way. After breakfast, he and Edwin insisted on being the ones to prepare Lord Thorne for his wedding. Roger appeared both suspicious and relieved, and Jacob didn't argue, saying he had no interest in being around Thorne if he could help it, as the wedding would probably have him on edge.

If Thorne was already irritable, he might send them away and ruin their plans. Marcus would do anything to stroke Thorne's ego if that's what it took to ensure that didn't happen.

Outside of Thorne's room, Marcus patted his belt, checking yet again that the small vial was safely tucked underneath it. Edwin patted his own stomach, confirming he had the rope. They were as prepared as they could be, but it provided little comfort.

If Marcus couldn't convince Thorne to drink something or was caught tampering with Thorne's drink, or if Alban's sleeping draught didn't work, their plan might not only fail, but Thorne might kill him and Edwin. Thorne wouldn't even be blamed if he claimed they were trying to murder him.

Marcus's courage wavered, but he straightened his spine and knocked. It was worth the risk—to protect Adriana, and to achieve the dream of their future together.

"You're late!" Thorne shouted.

In a bad mood already, then.

Wincing, Marcus opened the door. Thorne stood near the fireplace with his back to them, wearing a long dressing robe, his hair as perfect as ever, in the exact same braids he always wore. The silver hair stick glinted in the candlelight from the candelabras. Marcus and the others had theorized the hair stick was a simple enchantment that created an illusion of specific features.

If they were wrong, they'd have to use one of the worst backup plans.

Marcus entered with his hands folded in front of him and his head bowed. Edwin eased the door closed behind them.

"My lord—"

"You!" Thorne snarled. He dashed across the room and seized Marcus's chin. With a painful grip, he forced Marcus to lift his head. "What do you think you're doing here?"

"Serving you!" Marcus let all of his fear about what would happen if their plans failed bleed into his tone and expression. "I want to atone for my indiscretions, my lord. I am sorry."

Beside him, Edwin dropped to his knees. "My brother and I know we've displeased you," he said, a believable quaver to his voice. "We wish to help you prepare for the wedding cere-mony to demonstrate our dedication to loyally serving you."

Thorne eyed Edwin with a bit of smugness. "Do you now?"

"We're grateful for your magnanimity in giving us a place

in your esteemed household," Marcus said. "We only desire to humbly serve you on this joyous day. But if you wish to beat us and send us away for our presumption, that is your right, my lord."

The upward curl of Thorne's mouth was positively gloating as he released Marcus's chin. "Yes," he said softly, "it is my right."

His punch crashed into Marcus's abdomen, and Marcus stumbled back into the closed door with a gasp. Edwin clenched his fists but didn't move.

"Bow, then." Thorne sneered. "Prove to me you understand your place."

"Yes, my lord." Marcus doubled over in a bow.

"Lower."

Gritting his teeth, he knelt beside Edwin.

"Lower. Both of you."

In his mind, Marcus called Thorne every epithet he knew, but he bowed until his forehead touched the carpet. Edwin did the same beside him.

"Look at me."

Marcus looked up to find Thorne crouching before him, holding the silver hair stick in his human hand.

He flexed his scale-covered hand, then placed a claw under Marcus's chin. "Be a meek, perfect little servant, then. This is your last chance."

Marcus gulped. The sensation of his throat bobbing against the sharp tip of Thorne's claw made sweat form on the back of his neck. "Yes, my lord."

CHAPTER 22

Adriana twisted back and forth in front of her vanity mirror, admiring her reflection. Leena beamed at her, her hands clasped over her heart.

"Oh, Your Highness! You look like a dream!"

"Thank you."

She shifted again, enjoying the play of the light in the tiny glass beads sewn onto the fabric belt of the eggshell-blue gown. White sleeves were fitted to her arms, while eggshell fabric flowed down from bands on her upper arms that were also studded with glass beads. The skirt swished around her legs and a short train trailed after her, and a silver circlet set with five glittering diamonds rested on her forehead. Leena had taken extra time with Adriana's curls, and they were the closest to ringlets she'd ever managed to make them, the hair oil making them soft and luscious.

A girlish blush crept into her cheeks. Would Marcus also think she looked beautiful? She hoped so. Thinking of Marcus made her stomach clench. So many things could go wrong—

A firm, loud knock sounded on the door. It was time.

Adriana's heart felt like it was trying to crawl into her throat as she turned toward the door. Leena paused with her hand on the door handle and looked back at Adriana, only opening the door when she nodded.

The door swung open to reveal a group of people clustered in the hallway, all dressed in their finest tunics and gowns. Lucien Thorne stood at the head of the procession, an aloof expression on his face and his silver hair stick protruding from the back of his braids as always. Her mouth went dry, and she had to force herself to remain calm. This was the plan—unless something had gone wrong.

Father and Jairus flanked her groom, and Jairus chewed on his lower lip as he observed Lucien from the corner of his eye. Behind them, two knights and ladies watched, serving as the bridal escort—traditionally to ensure the bride and groom neither ran away nor were kidnapped or replaced en route to the wedding.

Adriana resisted the urge to wipe her clammy hands on her skirt as she crossed the room. *Please have worked, please—*

Lucien's gaze fell on her, and his jaw went slack. His eyes filled with a familiar, tender longing, and . . . were those tears? Either it had worked, or Lucien was shockingly emotional about marrying her. But which was it?

He cleared his throat. "You look beautiful, Adriana." It

wasn't quite Lucien's voice, more like someone mimicking Lucien, but it was close enough. If she hadn't been expecting him *not* to be Lucien, she likely wouldn't have noticed. Still, the cautious part of her didn't dare believe yet. Not until he'd confirmed it.

Lucien stepped into the room, holding out his arm to her. His boot knocked into the small stand beside the door, sending the potted gooseberry on it crashing to the ground. He startled, then bent forward to peer at the mess of dirt, broken pottery, and mangled leaves.

"Ah. Forgive me, little plant. I didn't notice you in my haste." He turned back to Adriana and winked. "I'll get you another."

A full smile broke onto her face, tears of joy threatening her own eyes, and she gladly took Marcus's arm. It was worth sacrificing her plant for the secret message that told her the plan was working.

They headed down the hall in a procession—Father in front, then Adriana and Marcus, magically disguised as Lucien thanks to the enchanted hair stick, Jairus behind them, and the four witnesses bringing up the rear. When they reached the winding tower stairs, Marcus spoke loudly enough for it to carry to the witnesses.

"Careful on the steps. Stairs, please don't trip us."

Father glanced over his shoulder with a frown, then shrugged. Adriana exchanged an amused smile with Marcus, although it was uncomfortable to look at Lucien's face at her side.

They descended the spiral staircase and continued down the hallway until they approached the massive oak door that led into the great hall.

"Allow me, Your Majesty," Marcus-as-Lucien said. He slipped his arm free of her hand and went around her father to grasp the large ring handle. As he tugged, the hinges gave a quiet squeal. "Ah, don't protest, door. It's my wedding day."

Father cast her groom a baffled look while Adriana stifled a laugh, and then he went through the door. Marcus took her arm again, and they entered the great hall. The tables were full of knights and their families, and many of the castle's servants stood near the walls. More candles had been brought in, so the room was as bright as noon on a clear summer day. Everyone watched them walk down the center of the hall to the dais on the far end, stopping just before the table.

Father stood in front of them, facing the hall, and Jairus moved to Adriana's left while the two knights and two ladies who had served as their witnesses sat at the tables. In the light of all the candles, the precious gems on the points of Father's crown appeared to glow.

"Face each other, kneel, and take each other's hands," Father said, his voice booming over them.

Marcus and Adriana did so. It was unnerving, kneeling there and looking into Lucien's blue eyes. How she wished she could do this across from Marcus with his own appearance. But he gave her hands a gentle, reassuring squeeze.

Father recited a traditional wedding rite, something about protecting and caring for and serving each other, but Adriana found it difficult to listen. Most of her mind was consumed with joy that this was happening—after all these years, after losing him twice and believing he was gone forever, she was marrying Marcus. But a small corner of her mind was afraid. Afraid this was too good to be true, and it really was Lucien across from her. Afraid that somehow things would still go wrong in a myriad of ways, and Marcus would be stolen from her again.

But then Marcus-as-Lucien said, "I so promise," and silently mouthed, "I, Marcus."

"And do you, Adriana Faine," Father said, "promise to love, cherish, and give yourself to this man and none other?"

"I so promise." She smiled, blinking back happy tears.

"Then I, by right as the father of the bride and the king of Aedyllan, pronounce this man and this woman to be husband and wife. You may rise and kiss the bride."

They stood and Marcus released her hands to grab her waist and pull her in. With her eyes closed, Adriana could have gotten lost in that kiss, but it looked like she was kissing Lucien—the man she'd begged Father not to force her to wed. So she quickly broke off the kiss. Marcus smiled, thankfully looking unoffended and unconcerned, and they turned and walked back through the cheering audience, their hands clasped between them.

As they headed up the stairs, butterflies filled Adriana's stomach. She'd been dreading this part of getting married when she was going to wed Lucien Thorne, but now . . .

"We're supposed to go to my room," Marcus whispered. "But obviously that's not going to work."

"I don't think anyone will notice, other than Leena, but she already knows and won't be in my room," she murmured back.

When they reached her room, the potted plant had been cleaned up and removed, a large bowl of fresh water and clean cloths had been placed on the vanity, and the fire had been built up, making the room cozily warm. Adriana bolted the door, and when she turned around, Marcus was standing before her as himself. He kicked aside the discarded hair stick, and the silver glittered as it spun across the carpet before disappearing into a dark corner.

Marcus still wore the same formal eggshell-blue tunic that matched her gown, and with the enchantment removed, it was baggy on him. Despite that, it was much more appealing on his slenderly muscular build than on Lucien, and paired better with his pale complexion, waist-length black hair, and brown eyes.

Or maybe she was just hopelessly attracted to Marcus.

"Your eye looks improved," she said, suddenly feeling a little shy.

Marcus smoothed his hands over his clothing. "Adriana . . . wife." His voice dropped low and husky, making her skin tingle. "I should warn you . . . I'm . . . slightly battered still. Beneath the tunic."

She stifled her disappointment and focused instead on her concern as she stepped closer to him and laid a hand gently on his chest. "Oh. We don't necessarily have to . . ."

"I want to," he declared, a smoldering passion in his eyes. "It's not very painful. I just didn't want you to be surprised. And . . . only if you're ready."

"This was my idea, husband." She gave him a sultry grin and was satisfied to see the way his throat corded and his hand flexed at his side. "I'm ready if you are."

With a feral smirk, Marcus looped his arm around her and yanked her against his chest. Their lips crashed together, the heat between them burning fiercer than the wood in the fireplace. It was like being devoured and given life at once, and she couldn't think of anything more than how much she loved this man who had loved her through every hardship and stayed faithful no matter how impossible things appeared. And now he was hers, and she would never let him go.

CHAPTER 23

Marcus drifted in a sea of hazy contentment. One hand lazily played with Adriana's curls, the other tucked under his head. His wife—his *wife*, to even think it made him feel like he could walk on air or fight a thousand armies—lay on her side, snuggled against him.

"We should get up and find your brother," he said reluctantly.

Adriana sighed. "Do we have to yet? I'm so comfy . . ."

"Think how much more pleasant this will be once Thorne is dealt with once and for all," Marcus pointed out as he scooted away from her. He fished his clothes off the floor and started dressing, stopping to lift an eyebrow at Adriana, who hadn't moved. "So just the bed was comfortable? And here I thought it was me."

She smiled, one side of her lips pulling up slightly higher than the other. "No, I'm enjoying the view."

"Mmm, no flirting when we have things to do," he said with a laugh.

Sighing, Adriana pushed off the bed and pulled her dress back on, although she didn't bother with tying on the drapey part of the sleeves. "Do up the laces for me, please?" she asked as she came around to his side of the bed and turned her back to him.

"Of course . . . how do I do this?"

She laughed. "Start at the top and work down, pulling the excess tight."

"Got it—"

A pounding on the door made the wood shake. Adriana sucked in a breath, and Marcus went rigid. This wasn't the plan—not the "if all goes well" plan, at least.

"Open this door!" King Mortimer's voice roared from the hall.

Adriana looked at him over her shoulder, and he found his own panic reflected in her eyes. This *definitely* wasn't the plan.

With a splintering of wood, the door burst apart. Thorne barged inside, his half-reptilian face contorted in fury. He must have awoken from the magical sleeping draught Marcus had slipped into Thorne's drink—and then somehow escaped the ropes that Edwin had so securely tied.

Marcus shoved Adriana back and stepped in front of her. He would not let that monster touch her.

"Nothing illicit between you and the princess, was it?" Thorne snarled. He seized Marcus by the throat and dragged him forward while Adriana screamed for him to stop.

King Mortimer and Prince Jairus entered, Jairus looking alarmed and Mortimer appearing as if steam were about to pour from his ears.

"As I suspected!" Thorne threw Marcus to the ground before the king. "After conspiring with the princess and hiding in my chamber to curse me when I arrived with my bride, this miscreant servant took the princess and came here and had his way with her!"

Coughing, Marcus pushed to his knees. "That's not—"

"Silence!" Thorne grabbed a fistful of Marcus's long hair. "With your permission, Your Majesty, I'd like to behead this depraved servant of mine—"

"No!" Adriana rushed at Lucien, but Jairus intercepted her and held her back.

"I suspect his death will break the vile curse he's placed on me," Thorne declared.

"I'd like to hear Marcus and Adriana's side of the story," Jairus said, his tone icy.

Thorne laughed and gave another eye-watering tug on Marcus's hair. "You'll accept the word of a base servant and a woman above that of a lord?"

"You're right," Jairus said. Adriana started to protest, but he cut her off. "If we're giving greater weight to an individual's testimony based on rank, I say again—I wish to hear Prince

Marcus Alimer's side of the story."

King Mortimer's face turned a darker shade of red, almost purplish. "You . . . I should have known."

Thorne's grip on his hair lessened. "What?"

"I didn't serve in the Alimer household," Marcus said. "I am Marcus Alimer, youngest son of Prince Arlius Alimer. Lord Thorne's story is a complete fabrication, and I can prove it."

He raised his chin, attempting to appear regal and confident despite kneeling on the floor while Thorne grasped his hair. "But I refuse to say another word until we have an audience, including the knights and ladies who served as the wedding party escort, as I claim the right to a public hearing."

Mortimer scowled. "You concealed your identity to infiltrate my castle, curse my guest, and steal my daughter—"

"I didn't curse . . ." Marcus shook his head. "As I said. I invoke the right to a public hearing for personal grievances that affect or involve the liege lord and will not say more—"

"You'd have to be my subject to invoke that right."

"I am, Your Majesty." Marcus attempted to bow, but it was nearly impossible with Thorne holding his hair. "I'm Aedyllanian. You're the king of Aedyllan. I was a subject of my father, and like all former subjects of Prince Arlius, I am now your subject since Alimer Principality was rightfully conquered by you and all within its lands claimed as yours."

"He's also my husband," Adriana said. "And that makes

him your subject."

"As crown prince," Jairus said, "I claim Marcus Alimer as under my protection and plead on his behalf for a public hearing."

The king ground his teeth. "I don't recognize him as Adriana's husband. But very well." His gaze flicked between Marcus and Adriana. "Bring them both to the great hall. Everyone is still there for the feast."

"May we finish getting dressed, Father?" Adriana asked, red creeping into her cheeks.

Mortimer eyed her. "You may. He is fine."

At least Marcus had his trousers and tunic on, so he was decent, if a little pathetic with bare feet and no belt. Adriana's unlaced dress hung awkwardly on her, the shoulders slipping off.

Leena slipped inside—she must have noticed the commotion and been watching in the hall. Her face was pale as she slunk over to Adriana.

"Jairus!" Mortimer glared at his son. "A word." He spun on his heel and strode out of the room. Jairus squared his shoulders and lifted his chin before following his father.

Thorne tugged sharply upward on Marcus's hair. "Get up." The moment Marcus was standing, Thorne yanked on his hair, pulling his head back. He whispered in Marcus's ear, "I'll kill you and your brother—or friend or whatever he really is. Wherever he's hiding, I'll find him, and neither of you will get away with this. Testify that you did curse me, that this was all a conspiracy against me, and I'll be merciful. Edwin will live, I won't punish Adriana for her part in this, and I'll kill you quickly."

He released Marcus's hair and shoved him forward. "Move."

Thorne pushed and manhandled Marcus all the way to the great hall, nearly knocking him down the stairs more than once. By the time they were standing in front of the dais, facing the buzzing crowd, his feet bore scrapes from the stone. Between making love and Thorne's yanking, his hair was tangled and mostly unbraided. But he stood tall anyway—until Thorne roughly shoved him to his knees.

The knights, ladies, their families, and the servants filling the great hall spared him little more than a glance, their horrified attention fixed on Thorne and his reptilian disfigurement.

Several moments later, Adriana and Jairus entered the hall. Her dress had been properly laced and her belt tied in place, and she at least wore her boots. She hadn't attempted to tame her disheveled curls. They hurried over to stand next to Marcus, opposite from Thorne.

Marcus smiled, trying to ease the fear written all over her face. Her returned smile was wobbly, but she also turned toward the audience with her head held high.

"We are here," King Mortimer said, "to settle a personal

grievance between Lord Lucien Thorne, Marcus Alimer, former prince of Alimer Principality, and myself."

The murmuring in the crowd rose to a roar, then abruptly cut off as the king motioned for silence.

"Lord Thorne. Please give your testimony of events."

Thorne wove a fabricated tale of Marcus purposefully deceiving his way into Thorne's household with the intent of framing Thorne and kidnapping Adriana. According to Thorne, Marcus had hidden in Thorne's bedchamber. When he arrived with Adriana after the wedding ceremony, Marcus had attacked Thorne, knocking him unconscious, tying him up, and cursing Thorne to his current monstrous appearance. Then Marcus had stolen his silver hair stick and enchanted it so he could disguise himself as Thorne and had taken Adriana. Marcus's plan, Thorne claimed he suspected, was to get Thorne killed and steal his life as Lord Thorne.

By the end of his tale, the crowd had turned their shocked, horrified, and disgusted stares on Marcus. He refused to cower under their judgment—he knew the truth.

"And what is your story, Marcus Alimer?" Mortimer asked in an icy tone.

"Rise and give your account, Marcus," Jairus said, an intensity in his eyes that dared his father to object.

Marcus stood, wincing a bit as his scraped feet brushed against the stone.

He began his story with coming to Glenborough to learn news of the woman he loved and his heartbreak at hearing of her engagement. His skin heated as he admitted to talking himself out of risking his life to contact Adriana and how he'd taken the first offer of employment he found. Jairus's nose wrinkled when he described the unfair terms of the contract.

Marcus told of his surprise when he realized where his new position was taking him, of the bittersweet joy of learning Adriana still loved him, and about discovering Lucien Thorne's true physical condition. In brief summary, he explained about planning to reveal the truth with Adriana, Edwin, and Jairus.

"So before the wedding, Edwin and I used a medicine supplied by Healer Alban to render Thorne unconscious, stole his enchanted hair stick, and were relieved when it transformed me to look exactly like Thorne—"

"Lies!" Thorne interrupted. "Alimer knew it would make him look like me because *he* enchanted it! I'm sure Prince Jairus believes his story, but until today, I didn't look like this—"

"So you claim that you performed the marriage ceremony with Adriana?" Marcus asked calmly.

"Of course I did. You may have stolen her to your bed, but as that is only half of the rite, legally she is unwed to either of us—"

"What if I can prove that I performed the marriage ceremony?"

"You can't." Thorne sneered. "You can't prove it was you any more than I can prove it was me."

Marcus turned to the audience. "Where are the marriage witnesses?"

The four men and women stepped out of the crowd. Marcus faced Adriana. "Your Highness, would you like to ask Thorne and me anything to prove which of us was with you from your room to the end of the marriage ceremony?"

Adriana smirked. "Lord Lucien. If you married me earlier today, then what did you say to my potted plant?"

"What?" Thorne's eyebrows drew together as his upper lip curled. "What kind of question is that? I didn't speak to a potted plant."

King Mortimer frowned, while the rite witnesses shook their heads.

She looked to Marcus. "What did my groom say to my potted plant?"

"I'm afraid I kicked over a potted plant in my bride's room, and then I said, 'Ah. Forgive me, little plant. I didn't notice you in my haste.' Then I promised Adriana that I'd replace it."

The witnesses nodded and murmured their agreement. Thorne worked his jaw, while the king appeared to waver between understanding and confusion.

"Lord Lucien," Adriana said. "If you are my groom, tell me what you said to the stairs."

"The stairs?" Thorne's hands clenched at his sides. "The . . . I . . . I said, 'I'm sorry we must step on you, stairs.'"

A knight among the witnesses snorted while the others shook their heads. Jairus grinned, and King Mortimer sighed, his expression resigned.

Marcus smiled. "I said, 'Stairs, please don't trip us.'"

"That's right," the witnesses muttered.

"Finally, Lord Lucien," Adriana said, triumph lighting her eyes, "what did you say to the door into the great hall?"

Lucien turned red as he opened and closed his mouth. "I asked it to let us in—"

"No," Marcus interrupted. "The hinges squeaked, and I said, 'Don't protest, door. It's my wedding day.'"

The witnesses muttered among themselves as a look of tired resignation crossed the king's face. One of the knights stepped forward and declared in a loud voice, "It is our sacred duty to confirm the bride and groom. While we were fooled by magic into believing that the groom was Lord Lucien Thorne, we can confirm the man who performed the marriage ceremony never left Princess Adriana's side. And we can further confirm the groom was Marcus Alimer, by virtue of his testimony."

"Thank you." Marcus gave a small bow. "By wedding ceremony and subsequent consummation, my marriage to Adriana Faine is sealed and recognized by the witnesses here and in the heavens."

He shared a warm smile with Adriana before turning slightly to better face the king. "Your Majesty. Lucien Thorne has sworn that I replaced him after he performed the marriage rites. As he was dishonest in this, I believe we can confirm that his entire story is a lie. But rather than accepting my word alone, I believe there may be another who can confirm my story—one who has no personal interest in me."

Jairus nodded and motioned toward the large door in the side of the hall. A servant pushed it open, and a knight and Edwin entered, escorting Roger between them.

The moment Roger's gaze landed on Thorne in his current half reptilian state, he turned an ashy shade of white, and then his complexion took on a greenish cast.

"It wasn't me!" Roger shrieked. "Lord Thorne, I didn't reveal you—"

"Silence!" Thorne's face contorted as he took a threatening step forward. "Don't speak another word."

"Why not?" King Mortimer asked. "What don't you want this servant to say?"

"Your Majesty," Marcus said. "This servant, Roger, has been with Lord Thorne the longest of any of his servants. If any of them know the truth about his condition, I wager it's him."

Roger wrung his hands, his eyes bulging as he glanced between Thorne and the king, weighing his options.

"Tell us what you know of how your lord came to look like

this," King Mortimer commanded.

Roger gulped and eased back a step, but Edwin pushed him forward again.

"I suppose he has threatened your life if you expose the truth?" Jairus asked gently. "I promise you on my honor as crown prince, if you tell the truth now, your life will be spared. If you refuse to speak, you will be held in contempt of the crown and executed."

Roger dropped to his knees. "I . . . I'll tell you—"

Thorne snarled and moved toward Roger, but the knight drew his sword and pointed the tip at Thorne's chest. Within moments, other swords were drawn around the great hall.

"He broke a deal with a fae," Roger blubbered. "Lord Thorne captured a fae in a trap. He made a bargain for strength and prowess in battle, and in exchange, he was to release the fae and grant the fae an acre of any lands he was awarded for his help on the battlefield. I don't know what the fae wanted the land for; all I know is when the fae came to claim his land two weeks ago, Lord Thorne refused. Because he kept only half of his word, half of his appearance was cursed. Lord Thorne agreed to sign over the acre of land in exchange for looking normal again, but after Lord Thorne signed the deed and handed it over, the fae gave him an enchanted silver hair stick—saying he'd promised only that he would make Lord Thorne *look* normal, not actually *be* normal."

Now the king's glare of fiery rage turned toward Thorne. "You lied to me, repeatedly deceived me, your king and planned father-in-law. You falsely accused an innocent man, threatened death and punishments to your servants outside of the bounds of the law, and broke a fae bargain, proving that you are an untrustworthy miscreant and not a man of your word. I revoke your title and your lands. For knowingly lying to the king in a grievance hearing and attempting to cause the execution of an innocent man, I hereby sentence you to death."

"No!" Thorne flexed his clawed, scale-covered hand. "This servant is lying! They're both lying! I—"

"Take him outside and behead him," King Mortimer ordered. "I don't want to see that wicked monstrosity a moment longer."

Several knights converged on Thorne and dragged him, flailing and screaming obscenities, out of the hall.

The door slammed shut, blocking out Thorne's deranged protests. Marcus finally let himself relax, and Edwin grinned at him. All of their planning and risks had paid off, but Thorne had been so confident in his lies Marcus had feared he would convince Adriana's father and their witnesses.

Marcus bowed to King Mortimer. "Your Majesty. Thank you for seeing that justice is done." He straightened. "As your humble subject, I ask you—do you recognize my marriage to Princess Adriana, whom I dearly love?"

Mortimer's mouth pinched as he glanced over the waiting crowd. Marcus held his breath as the king delayed answering. Surely he wouldn't forbid them from being together. The entire point of standing in as Lucien during the marriage ceremony and demanding this hearing be in public was so the king couldn't deny the existence of the marriage and quietly have him killed.

"Adriana performed the wedding ceremony with the knowledge it was Marcus Alimer, not Lucien Thorne," Jairus said solemnly. "They will both admit to consummating the marriage, and we . . ." He coughed. "Based on the state we found them in, I believe we can attest that their marriage was formalized."

Marcus willed his face not to turn red as Adriana blushed. As much as he'd enjoyed that and looked forward to doing it again, he could do without Adriana's brother discussing it in front of a room full of strangers.

"I acknowledge that Marcus Alimer and my daughter are legally wed," Mortimer said tightly. "But there are other concerns. You deceived me as well, Alimer, by concealing your true identity within my castle and then impersonating Thorne in the wedding rite. You and your servant"—he motioned at Edwin—"infiltrated my castle and proceeded to undermine my authority by stealing my daughter—"

"I was not stolen!" Adriana protested. "You would have

given me to a man I did not love and who did not love me and wasn't even a good man! And what recourse did you leave Marcus after you sent an assassin to kill him?"

"An assassin who lied to me," the king muttered.

Edwin cleared his throat. "I faked my prince's death, Your Majesty. Your knight was not dishonest with you."

Marcus winced. He'd tried to convince Edwin to stay hidden until everything was settled and run if things went wrong, but of course his friend wouldn't listen.

"Another count of deception—"

"Father," Jairus said pleadingly. "You tried to have Marcus killed because you feared he would retaliate against you for the deaths of his family or might stir up opposition to your rule. But Marcus has been in Faine Castle for days and caused no harm, and in fact took great risks to himself to protect Adriana from marriage to a monster. He did not attempt to murder you or me, and he married your daughter because he loves her, not because he wants anything from you. He has assured me that he holds no ill intent toward you for acts performed in a war his own father started. He has no desire for the throne and is willing to publicly take oaths of fealty to you."

Marcus dropped to one knee before the king. Enough letting others defend him. If he wanted to fight for his dreams, he needed to take the risks himself.

"Your Majesty." He bowed his head. "I acknowledge that

I deceived you. I also swear I bear you no malice and harbor no aspirations of kingship—I'd happily live out my days as an untitled farmer in a cottage with Adriana at my side. I have said I consider myself your subject, and as such, I accept that my fate is entirely in your hands. I trust that you are a good man and noble king and will do what is right. Do with me what you believe is just. I ask only three things of you."

Marcus raised his head to meet Mortimer's gaze. "Allow my servant, Edwin, to live. He acted under my instructions and any fault lies with me alone. Remember your love for your daughter and do not punish her or force her into another marriage. And if you truly believe that justice demands my death . . ." His chin quivered, and he had to swallow back his fear. "Don't let my wife watch. Please."

The king's expression softened, the anger and distrust gradually replaced by something more like regret and acceptance. The rest of the hall seemed collectively to hold their breath.

Adriana's eyes glistened with unshed tears as she stepped closer. "Father, please—"

Mortimer held up his hand to silence her without taking his assessing gaze off of Marcus. "Then you will here, before all these witnesses, swear your fealty to me and that neither you nor your descendants shall ever challenge my rule or the rule of my heirs?"

Placing his right fist over his heart, Marcus bowed while

still kneeling. "I, Marcus Alimer, have always longed for peace in Aedyllan. I swear on the stars in the sky, the blood in my veins, and the ancient soil beneath my feet my fealty and allegiance to King Mortimer Faine, and promise that I will always support his rule and the rule of his heirs, and shall instruct my descendants to always honor their oaths of fealty to the Faine line, for so long as you and your descendants rule the people of Aedyllan justly and protect the peace of Aedyllan."

King Mortimer nodded gravely. "I accept your allegiance and your declaration of our most sacred oath, Marcus Alimer. On the virtue of your actions and the testimony of others to your character, I recognize you as my son-in-law and Adriana Alimer's husband, and I grant you the title of duke and bequeath you the lands formerly held by Lucien Thorne. You may rise."

A cheer went up from the crowd, Edwin's whoop the loudest of all. When Marcus looked over at his wife, it was to see Adriana applauding while tears of joy slipped down her cheeks. The moment he was on his feet, she ran to him, colliding with his chest as she threw her arms around him. He wrapped her in a return embrace, pulling her close. How was it possible to love someone so much that he couldn't ever hold her close enough to convey the depth of his devotion?

"I'll always love you," he said as he leaned his cheek against the side of her head. "I am your husband, as I once vowed I would be, and I swear by the same sacred oath—by the stars, my blood, and the very ground—I will never leave you. I'll always be there when you need me, so far as is in my power, my darling, beloved Adriana."

Her arms tightened around him, and then she pulled back and met his eyes. "And I'll always love you. I swear it on the stars in the sky and the blood in my veins and the ancient soil beneath my feet, my husband, my beloved Marcus."

"And I promise to never give up on the dream of us," Marcus said.

He would not lose hope again, and this time, his dreams wouldn't be built on castles made of clouds.

Marcus would act on his hope that their future would be bright and full of love. He would love and support Adriana every day. He would treat his subjects well and use his power as duke and the king's son-in-law to defend the peace and prosperity of Aedyllan with Adriana as his partner and ally.

At long last, without fear of being seen, Marcus bent down and kissed Adriana with all the passion of years of longing, all the boundless depths of his dedication, and the tenderness of the promise of many years to come.

THE END

Author Note

While injuries and wound care depicted in this book were researched, the depictions are fictional, and nothing in this book should be interpreted or used as medical advice.

Get a Marcus & Adriana Spotify playlist
when you subscribe to Selina's newsletter!
Plus be in the know for when future books release.
SelinaRGonzalez.com/newsletter-subscription

The Miraveld Chronicles

Other books set in the same world, 200 years later.
Can be read as standalones but work best if you start with book one.

Find out what happens when a vengeful witch sets out to end the fae blessing bestowed on the Faine line in book 3, *A Fated Quest*!

A Thieving Curse (The Miraveld Chronicles book 1)
A princess on her way to an arranged marriage is caught by an exiled prince with a dragon shifter curse, endangering a treaty and her heart in this reimagining of *Beauty and the Beast.*

A Lonely Dance (The Miraveld Chronicles book 2)
Can a man who sees himself as a villain unworthy of affection help a princess caught in a curse—without losing his heart or his life in this reimagining of *Twelve Dancing Princesses?*

A Fated Quest (The Miraveld Chronicles book 3)
A deceptively simple quest leads a prince on an adventure with a talking fox, a sword-wielding damsel, a stubborn unicorn, and a vengeful witch. Inspired by *The Golden Bird* and *Tsarevich Ivan, the Firebird, and the Gray Wolf.*

A Stolen Heart (The Miraveld Chronicles book 4)
Blackmailed into infiltrating the palace, a former villainess fears redemption is out of reach—and the suspicious general who sees through her deception could be her doom or her salvation in this reimagining of *The Goose Girl.*

ACKNOWLEDGMENTS

First, thank you to Alora and Constance for organizing the Once Upon a Prince series and inviting me to take part! I am so honored to be included, and it has been so much fun to work with you guys and see this amazing series come together. Thank you for your beta reading feedback and helping me make this book stronger. Thank you to the rest of the authors in the series as well for making this such a fun experience.

Thank you to my early readers for all your help in making this book the best it can be: Mom, Alexis, Janice, Becky, and Kate (who is so wise in the ways of grammar).

Thank you to Anna A, Brigitte C, Cheyenne L, Constellation, Katelyn R, Laurel (Yanny), Michelle B, and Raqpunzel, who sent me suggestions for this book's playlist (way back when I shared only vague vibes for a Secret Project XD). Even though the songs didn't make it onto the playlist, it was so fun to listen to your suggestions! Extra thanks to Jenni for several suggestions that *did* make the cut, and to J.E. and Jenni (again—playlist queen) for suggestions that didn't make it onto *Crownless's* playlist but did end up on a future project's playlist!

Thank you to every reader who was excited for this book, who pre-ordered or read an ARC or cheered me on as I was working on this book.

And thank you, specifically, dear reader—thank you for reading Marcus and Adriana's story. Without you, pursuing my dream of being an author wouldn't be possible. ♥

Finally, thank you to my Author and Creator, my God who has been a refuge in storms over the last few years, even when I struggled to feel Your wings around me.

About the Author

Selina R. Gonzalez is a Colorado native with mountains in her blood and dreams that top 14,000 feet. She loves chocolate, fantasy, costumes, bread, history, superheroes, faux leather, things that sparkle, medieval Britain, snark, dogs, and Jesus—not in that order.

Find bonus content, keep up to date on all the latest news from Selina, and don't miss any of Selina's future books by subscribing to her newsletter at:

SelinaRGonzalez.com/newsletter-subscription

www.ingramcontent.com/pod-product-compliance
Lightning Source LLC
Chambersburg PA
CBHW061806190726
48289CB00007B/2097